PAULA'S PLACE

Seduction, Surrender, Submission

JAMES WOOD

Paula's Place: Seduction, Surrender, Submission
Copyright © 2013 by James Wood.

Edited by Sharazade for 1001 Nights Press.

Cover design by CoverDomme.
Printed in the United States.

ISBN-13: 978-0615772738

ISBN-10: 0615772730

Table of Contents

PART 1:
SEDUCTION

Chapter 1
Grand Falls

I WRITE THIS AS A TESTAMENT to a time I will never forget. Little did I think, when I returned to Grand Falls, that my life would utterly change. Where once I was hollow, now I am full. Where I doubted of the existence of love, now it holds me tight in its grip. I am no longer the innocent girl; I am blissful, complete, and knowing. He has opened my eyes to the world. I am his and I have flowered.

Yet before you can hope to understand of what I speak, we must return to the beginning. Back to when I stepped from the train into the town where I grew up.

"IS THAT EVERYTHING, PAULA?"

Aunt Emily, who had looked after me always, meant no meanness by her question. She tried vainly to hide the concern she must have felt over my request to come and stay with her – in the circumstances there had been very little notice. We traded kisses on the cheek as we'd done since I was a child.

"Yes, Em. Just the suitcase. I might go back and get a few things, but this is all I need for the moment." Just seeing her made me feel better.

Em tried not to pry on the ride home. I spared her by volunteering the story.

I had left him; that's what happened. My life was not how it was meant to work out. We'd met at college and lived together in the city where I'd fought to start a career. The years ticked by; how does that happen? Looking back, I suppose I had been waiting for him to drop the question. I just assumed it would be that way.

"Definitely over then?" Em probed gently.

"I don't know what I saw in him. Wasted all those years." Em had something of a smile about her now and seemed much cheerier than she'd been since she collected me. "What? Now you're going to tell me you never liked him from the start?"

"Sometimes things work out for the best, dear. You can stay as long as you like."

I GOT MY OLD ROOM BACK. It had changed a bit since high school; Em had taken the posters down and had someone paint the walls.

"There are fresh towels in the closet. I'll go down and start on lunch."

Our house is on Vale Street, which isn't so

remarkable except that in Grand Falls that makes it old – our street being one of the very few to escape the town's big fire. Our house is a fine one, too. They call it a Gothic design. I'm never sure if "gothic" needs to be capitalized, but the house is so twisty and spired it deserves one regardless. Em takes a pride in its gardens. When I was growing up all my friends loved to play in it – so many good places to hide.

There is a park outside our house, one block wide and three long. It has been there forever. The trees are old and the shade is inviting on hot sticky summer days. I guess looking at that park I knew I was right to come back here and start again. That's what home is for. Em called me down and I went.

I DON'T KNOW WHAT BROUGHT IT ON. I hadn't had thoughts like that in years. I suppose it was seeing the park again, and it being my first night away from the city.

I had gone to bed. I had turned out the light after reading a bit, and the house was completely quiet. I had left the window open and through it could see the moon; its light fell over my sheets.

I lay back, keenly aware of the stirring in my body. I pulled my knees up so my feet lay flat and I let my knees fall open. I stretched my arms above my head and gripped the bed rail tightly. There was an awareness in my body, a growing murmur that needed satisfaction and would not go away. I didn't want it to. For the first time in a long time, I ached to be touched and held.

Sex had been one of the problems we'd had, I see that now. It was an unspoken thing at the end. It wasn't that we didn't do it, but I felt bad for wanting more. He'd always go on top. He wouldn't kiss me; I'd have liked that. One time I talked to him about things I'd like to try, but once proved one time too many. I didn't dare tell him of the dreams I had. He'd never have understood those. And so the years had passed.

There wasn't much of a breeze, but the window was open and the curtain gave a stir. I pushed the blanket off me and closed my eyes. I moved one hand onto my belly. He was coming again: The Colonel. I could feel him outside the window. I arched my back a little ways and pushed my hand between my thighs. I touched myself on top of my shorts and let out a silent moan.

The dream came in many disguises, but it always started within the park. It was back in the time of the Civil War, and I was out gathering wood for the house. We knew there was a battle looming nearby. I know I'd been told to be careful. Nevertheless, I walked on alone, hidden by trees, fearful for any noise.

In the bed, my right arm stretched high above my head. My fingers wrapped themselves around the bed rail and gripped it like in a storm. My left hand found my waistband and slipped underneath my shorts. With the material against the back of my hand

I parted my woman's curls.

There was someone there. I could hear the horse whinny and the underbrush snapping. "Whoa, girl." It was a man's voice, deep and soothing, calming the nervous beast. "What's got you all stirred up?" I was frozen, not knowing whether to run or hide, fearful of discovery at any time. I'd heard stories of rough men and what they did with honest women, and it paralyzed my mind. I could just make him out through the branches: an officer on a fine chestnut mare. His coat was dusty and I couldn't make out whether it was blue or gray. He saw me. He always saw me. And that's when I turned and ran.

I gasped as my fingers spread my lips and stroked the inside of my petals. I released the bed frame to grasp my breast and give myself a squeeze. *Oh, Paula, you dirty girl*, spoke my conscience. Only one night back and then this. But my mind was away with the pursuing Colonel, whose horse would soon overtake me.

I dropped my bundle and sprinted, dashing under branch and behind tree. But my skirts were long and the brush was difficult and I had little hope of escape. I could hear him now, right behind me, the beating of hooves closing in. I fell. I always fell. I started to crawl away.

"What do we have here?" He dismounted. Spurs jangling from his heels. His sword remained in the scabbard on his saddle but a pistol was at his waist. I crawled, frantic, on hand and knee. He took a sore grip of my dark curled hair just as I'd reached a fallen tree.

"Oh, sir. Please, sir, no!" I pleaded, but he put his hand on my mouth to stop me. I bit hard on his fingers only to find

11

he'd gagged me with a leather gauntlet. He took me then, he always took me, he pushed me down on that broken tree. He threw my petticoats over my waist and held my wrists behind my back to tame me.

"You're going to get it, girl. You're going to enjoy this. I'm going to fill your belly with my seed and drive you rough, like you're needing." Then he put his bare hand between my legs and felt me wet and swollen. He was momentarily surprised, always just for a moment. "You're no lady! Dirty girl. You're a filthy trollop. You want it, yes, I can feel it here, I've got the proof on my own fingers." And then he unbuttoned his cavalry breeches and unburdened himself into me.

Until now I had avoided my clitoris: tense and ripe and swollen. But at this point, as the Colonel mounted me, I gave it my full attention.

"Whore, that's what you are. Wanting a real man's attentions. I'll give it to you, hard as you like, that you'll be dreaming of me with your husband." He grabbed my hair, tight as cord, and pulled it till I was screaming. But only a muffled mew did I manage through the salty leather I bit on.

He drove me, his flared root invading my belly, over and over and over. He tore at my dress and spilled my breasts and twisted them sore, quite fiercely.

I was there now, my fingers juddering, my womb in spasm, my clitoris ripened to bursting. I lifted my back, my hips clear from the bed, with my breasts pinched by my own stealthy hand. He always came too at this point. He never failed to deliver.

"God. You. Bitch." He thrust desperately into me then, his breath in suspension; he pressed tightly inside me and

trembled. It was that way for moments. Finally, he withdrew. I could feel his semen dripping out of me, running down my thighs. It was undoubtedly collecting on my wool stocking tops, where it would stain them as evidence. He took out a knife and cut my underwear from me, leaving me naked to God. He removed his glove from between my teeth and released his hand from my wrists.

"There you go. You can tell anyone you like; they'll know what you are. And if you have a child, you bring him up well or I'll find you and give you a whipping."

He wiped himself on the hem of my dress and then buttoned himself up and mounted. "What's your name, whore?" he called down.

"Paula," I whispered. I had gathered myself up by now.

"You'll want it again, Paula, another time. I know you will. You know where you can find me." Then he left me standing alone; he pushed his horse into a canter.

I lay back, flat on the bed, the sheet beneath me damp with sweat. When the trembling stopped I stayed still for a while and listened to the street noise in the darkness. I felt a secret shame, but it was better for that. My secret. It felt wrong and yet right also. I changed into a clean, dry t-shirt and locked this puzzle in my mind away, and the next thing I knew it was morning.

Chapter 2
The Curious House

It was something like three weeks after my arrival that I was first drawn to the curious house. It was much like ours, a mirror almost, since it faced us across the park. I rarely had a need to walk that way, since the shops and town are east of us, but an anomaly in the way the streets were numbered would mean that we sometimes got their mail.

What happened that night had nothing to do with the mail. It was dark out, but too early for bed. Em and I were arguing over what to watch when there was a loud bang from outside, yet quite near. We couldn't see anything from the living room window, so I went upstairs for a better view. There was a car alarm going off too. There were some people on the street, down the block, but I couldn't make out what was happening. I had seen a pair of binoculars on the landing and went back down to fetch them. I killed the light in my bedroom to see better, but what I saw had me thinking for days.

I didn't mean to spy. I can say that honestly.

Not that first night, anyway.

When I took up the binoculars and focused them

in, I caught a glimpse of the house across the street. There, like a reflection of myself, stood a woman looking out, drawn to the noise on the street. But she was naked; leastways her bra had been pulled down, and a man dressed in black stood close behind her. I felt like a peeping Tom and rather shameful of my attentions, yet here was something that I couldn't pull my eyes from. It wasn't just that they were fooling around, but something different was going on. The woman had her hair pinned up and it was clear that she wore a collar. The man held a leash that was attached to it, as if he was walking a dog. He pulled on it as I watched on, and dragged her away from the window.

I could see when she turned that her arms were tied, secured by elaborate coils of rope. Then the man who had started to pull the drapes shut paused and looked my way and squinted. I gasped and pulled back, letting the binoculars drop – their house now seemed far off and dark.

"What's going on outside, Paula?" Em was calling up.

What were they doing? What game were they playing? Why did I feel so aroused?

"Just a car, I think." I made it up. "Fender bender, looks like."

"Well, they're disturbing the whole neighbour-hood."

Yes, they were.

AFTER THAT NIGHT I KEPT A VIGIL. I found my old telescope and its rickety tripod in the attic. Despite its advertisements, it had only ever been good for staring at the moon. This had disappointed me plenty in ninth grade. Now it found a new purpose.

"Who lives in that house opposite, Em? I don't remember there being any kids."

"Which one? In the middle? Beside that one, you mean? Oh, that's number 88. Some author figure bought it a few years back after old Mr. Singer passed on. Keeps to himself, much as I can hear. Mrs. Miller has been looking for a reason to complain about him, but he pays Dobson's boy to do his gardening. She says there are people that come and go at weekends, at weird times too, so she says. But a person's got a right to privacy if they want it, and she should keep her nose out of his business."

I knew Em didn't mean anything by her words, though she'd looked twice at me when I set up the telescope. I couldn't help feel a little guiltier then, seeing as how I'd been checking on him regularly. I was bored, you see – small towns have that way about them – and my imagination had been stirred by that first glimpse. What was the mysterious author up to? What games were being played?

While the leaves were still on the trees, I could only get a clear view of that very top room; the rest of the place was hidden. For the first few nights there was not so much as a light being turned on over there. It wasn't like I was obsessed with it, but I would check before going to bed. A strange thing had started happening to me, and I knew what the cause had been – the Colonel no longer visited me as I lay alone on my bed before sleeping. Instead there came a shadowy figure, a man who was dressed in black. He would chase me through the woods and into the house and catch me as I ran up the staircase. He would tie my arms behind my back. He would loop them together in elaborate strings that looked for all the world like spider web. Then the man in black would put a collar around my neck and lead me by a leash to his chamber. There he would chain me to his bed before he would strip me very slowly. Slowly. Taking his time. Unbuttoning my blouse. Knowing that I was helpless. Sensing a need inside of me that wouldn't let me cry out in alarm. Undoing every button. Then he would lean over me and …

I startled from my dream. I took my hand out from my panties because I'd seen a light appear. It was the room in the curious house across the street from me. My author had come back again.

I found myself trembling, though I didn't know why; it was the first time I'd seen him clearly. He was alone. He was trim and looked fit – I wasn't complaining – he seemed to be assessing the room. I judged him perhaps five years older than me, which surprised me – I'd pictured him older. He showed strong tanned forearms with his sleeves rolled up, and his arms bulged as he dragged a piece of furniture. His white shirt was tucked into stonewashed jeans that showed a tight hard ass as he wrestled it. His hair was thick and dark and slightly wild, which I had always found very attractive.

Oh, dear, Paula. This isn't good. I admonished myself for being superficial. *He's probably a complete asshole.* But I was touching myself regardless.

Finished with doing whatever he'd come for, he was now leaving the room. The light went out and I caught his silhouette in the doorway just before it closed. The light didn't come on again until Friday.

It was Friday when I was discovered.

WHEN THE LIGHT WENT ON, their window was blessedly open. My author had brought a woman with him, who wore a snug black dress and heels. She wasn't the same woman as before. I didn't know how that made me feel, but I was interested to know. I'd think about it later. He led her in, holding her hand, and closed the door behind them. In the darkness of my own room, I curled up in my blanket.

He pulled her to him and they embraced; the slut was all over his body. They went on like this for a minute or two, which only stirred my own need cruelly. Then, as I watched, he took over.

It was the way he held her, at first. His hands, which had roamed her sides and back, now slid up her arms and took hold of her. Slowly but firmly, with a hold of her wrists, he moved her arms behind her back. She looked weak in his grip, like she was floating. He held her wrists with one of his hands while he stroked her now with the other. He kissed her; not upon the mouth, but on her neck and down over her shoulder. Her head fell back as she gave herself up, and his hand touched her leg at her nylons. He turned her a little, so I couldn't see all, but I sensed that his hand was moving. She moved a little to the side and I could see her skirt ride up on her. I knew he was touching her intimately.

I couldn't help but join in; my fingers were frisky, imagining his hand was on me.

By now he had moved her against the far wall, to the spot that I'd seen him clear earlier. Then, to my amazement, he tied her hands and drew them up with a rope to the ceiling. I had to adjust the telescope. I had to see what was going on. He had passed the rope through something in the ceiling that held her arms in a gesture of surrender. She'd been tied up. There was nothing she could do. She couldn't push him away now even if she wanted to.

He turned her to face the wall; it could only be inches away. Now he was saying something into her ear and I saw her spread her feet.

I was swollen. I had a small vibrator I would sometimes use, but I didn't want or need it at this moment. I wanted the longing within my body to build and last as long as possible.

Now, only now did he undress her. He took an age to do it. He stroked her arms with gentle fingers before unfastening the straps at her shoulders. Then the zipper. He traced its fall with little kisses that he planted upon her spine, and when it reached her lower back he let her dress fall down to the floor.

I almost felt sorry for the woman – lucky girl that she was – she must have been squirming in those panties. I could see she'd come prepared for an amorous evening because of the lingerie she was wearing. It was black and sheer – the dirty floozy, tempting him with her bod. She wore black stockings that had a seam down the legs, held in place by an old-fashioned garter belt.

He said something else to her and she stuck out her ass, letting the rope take the weight of her body. He reached down under her now, his hand between her legs, and he seemed to be cradling her vulva.

I didn't know what to do. I was nearly there, but I had to see the end of this. I had pushed two fingers inside of myself; my palm firmly pressed to my labia. I was grinding on my hand as I touched my nipples, and I knew I would dissolve any minute.

Then my author turned. He looked my way as if he could see me in the darkness, impossible though that could be. When his window was dark, I could barely make out a thing, and that was with the telescope. But what if I had judged it wrongly? What if, that first night, he'd caught me peeking? Was he looking out here for me? Was this a show I'd been meant to watch? Was he deliberately showing me everything? Maybe the street lamps were different on this side and threw light in enough to reveal me.

I was momentarily shocked. I took my hands off

myself, as if discovered in my shame. I felt undressed and exposed.

There could be no doubt. He walked over to the window and instead of closing the drapes, he pulled them further back. *Have a good look.* Is that what he was saying? *Is this what excites you, my peeker?* Was he smiling?

He turned back to the helpless woman and slid her panties from her. He eased them past her garter belt and down over her nylons and heels. Her ass was exposed and I could imagine her womanhood: swollen and lustful and eager. He spoke to her again, and then he held her chin as he fed her those expensive panties. He had gagged her. She was made to hold her underwear inside her pretty mouth.

I was enraptured. Was he doing this for me? I renewed my attentions to my own desires, knowing the woman in the room could do nothing.

Then he took off his belt. She didn't struggle as he coiled it around his fist, so I expect she knew what was coming. The leather was thick and wide and loose; it hung down cruelly from his hand. He spoke once more and she stuck out her ass up high as he unbuttoned and rolled up his sleeve. He then reached around and touched her pussy, as if checking whether she was wet. He seemed satisfied. My author raised his arm slowly and then brought it down hard and fast. His victim flinched and bucked with pain but did not change her pose.

I flinched too. I was physically jarred. I couldn't

believe what I was seeing. When I found the viewer on the telescope again he'd already given her a few more – there were two or three red marks on her bottom, showing brightly against her skin.

He stopped for a moment and talked to her and held her pussy while he did so. Then he gave her some more, same as before, and I saw the pattern repeated. He would smack her with his leather belt, then touch her and talk close to her ear. Sometimes too he would bend down to kiss the marks that he had made. He caressed her ass, massaging his work, as if to soothe the heat of her skin. And all the while she hung from the ropes to which she was bound, immobilized. Though I could not hear the sounds they made, I empathized with her torment.

He stopped now – I had come long ago – and I watched as he unbuttoned himself. It was clear that he would now slake his desire in the woman he had bound for his pleasure. I didn't know if I could watch, I was so turned on yet burning jealous. In the end I didn't get the choice because he killed the light switch. I was left with my hand on the contours of my lips; I was tender and soaking and breathless.

THE NEXT DAY I SAW THAT BLINDS had been fitted to the window across the street, and what's more that the drapes were now drawn. It made me tremble because it confirmed my fears that he'd known of me all along. More embarrassing still, and shameful to acknowledge, I found myself wet at the thought.

Chapter 3
The Author of My Desires

It was my curiosity that led me to do such a risky thing, though frustration might be a better word. The house across the street once again fell silent, and the upper window remained blocked from my prying. In my own defense, I held out nearly four days before taking matters into my hands.

I was walking in the park – there was nothing wrong with that – and if I noticed that the author's house seemed quiet, then what of it? I notice lots of things. They had an outside mailbox and the flag was up. An outrageous idea occurred to me. I took a brief glance up and down the block – there was no one around to see me. Sometimes fate comes to you. Sometimes you step out and make it.

I opened the mailbox. There were a couple of letters and a handful of useless flyers. They were addressed to the same person: Mr. Maximilian Broekner. It sounded made up. I took the most important-looking one, sent from Walter Mitty Publishing. It was either a cheque or a bill, hard to tell, but I figured he'd be looking for either. I stuffed the rest back in the mailbox and put the letter into my pocket. It was just neighbourly to return mis-delivered mail. I now had an excuse to drop in on him.

I rang the doorbell. I rang it again. I knew it was a lost cause before the third time. I should have put the letter into my bag and tried my ruse again the next day, but for some reason that day I didn't. There was a little path around the side of the house that led off into the garden. I followed. It led, as I thought, to the back of the house, where a glass conservatory had been added to the building. Cacti and tropical plants all bloomed beneath its panes. There was no one home that I could see as I glanced in its many windows. I tried the door to the conservatory. It opened and let me in.

A grandfather clock made the only noise; I called out "hello" before going further. At first I hung back near the door till I was certain there weren't any dogs. Mr. Broekner must do okay. The place must have cost a bundle. It had hardwood floors, just like Aunt Em's, but it had to be double the size. The place was done in dark wood, the furniture Spartan but expensive-looking. The ceiling must have been twelve feet high and the whole place was open and welcoming. This surprised me. I was used to our house, Aunt Em's house, and its little rooms. Maybe upstairs was different? I wandered further, and as I did I started to feel a mite nervous. Now a letter in my bag wouldn't cut it; right now I was breaking and entering. Yet I felt the need to know more about this man, and I was drawn by the lure of his house. I was right about the clock – I found it standing at the bottom of the staircase. Up, up it went. I knew that at the top of those stairs there was a room where all those things I'd seen had happened. My heart was going fast. My lips were slightly parted, my breathing audible through my mouth. What if I heard someone coming in? What would I say or do?

I put my hand on the banister rail and carefully took the first step. I felt my throat tightening and a tingle of expectation. If anyone came in the front door now, I couldn't make it out the back before them. I told myself I'd only have a look. Just one look and then I'd be gone.

I found his study. That's what it had to be. It was the first room that I came to on the next floor of the house. There was still one more flight of stairs up. If I was going to find anything about this man, then surely it was here. A minute to have a look in his study and then upstairs to the top of the place. In less than five minutes, I promised myself, I'd be back outside and safe.

The image of him I held in my mind was one for which I wanted some confirmation. He had appeared as a black shadow the first time, pulling on that woman's collar. Then he was tousled dark hair and strong tanned arms when he whipped that tied-up woman. I felt Mr. Broekner becoming clearer; I felt I was getting closer. I looked, but there weren't any pictures. I was a little disappointed at that.

There were books. There were shelves and shelves of books. And there was one of those fancy Apple computers. I resisted turning it on. I looked instead at the titles on the shelves for a clue to the man I had seen. There were reference books and classical fiction but one shelf in particular drew my attention. On it was the sort of heated fiction I had leafed through for excitement. Some books were very familiar: Anaïs Nin's *Little Birds*, *Fanny* by Erica Jong, a great number of Henry Miller. *Nine and a Half Weeks* by Elizabeth McNeill and Anne Rice's *The Claiming of Sleeping Beauty*. I'd riffled through that as a teenager in the library, hiding away at the back. The whispered words, the intimate touching, the rope and collars and leash – all of these things seemed more present and real in the library Mr. Broekner was keeping.

I turned to leave when my attention was drawn to a slim book on the desk itself. It was a paperback, thin and fanned as if recently opened and read. I picked it up. *The Doctrine of Venus* by a Dr. Edgar Haldrew. I'd never heard of it before. It felt old, and its pages browned. The book fell open on a page discussing the rules for collaring your lover. There were explicit pictures. They looked Victorian, but they made me blush all the same. I put it down. Collaring your lover. Was that what Mr. Broekner was doing up there with those women? The stripped girl with the strap around her neck and her arms tied elaborately behind her back? Was she being collared? Whatever that meant. I felt a groan from inside my womb, a desire that went unmet.

I went back to the stairs.

Slowly, slowly now. Somehow as I got closer to that place, I had to creep inch-like to the edge. I went up the stairs as I might draw near a cliff, in awe of the majestic risk. I had my bearings, there was no doubt. The room in which I'd witnessed these things was right in front of me now. I reached a hand out to the handle and started to turn the knob.

There was a noise downstairs.

A door opened and then closed heavily. The front door! There was the loud tread of confident feet. Someone was here! Someone was home. I heard footsteps on the stairs approaching.

I froze. I didn't know what to do. I was terrified and shaking. I knew I would be seen from below if I stayed where I was any longer. I turned the handle and went into the room, closing the door behind me. I had nowhere else to hide! I was trapped in the place I'd come to see. I might be discovered at any time.

It was dark. The drapes were drawn, of course, but there was muted light to see by. I didn't dare try for the light switch. I crouched down behind the door and listened with my ear.

Someone was coming. He was coming! It had to be him.

What was I going to say to him, what could I do to explain? I was so scared and it reminded me suddenly of my time when the Colonel was there. I felt the same sense of panic, the frightened mouse in my chest. I didn't want to breathe for risk of discovery, but there was no way of escape I could see. If I didn't move, if I didn't make a sound, would the noise in the woods go away? What was I thinking? Why had I come here? Why was I there? And the noise didn't go away. The noise came closer and closer. My heart filled my throat and I thought I would faint as I heard footsteps mounting the stairs.

Paula, you fool, this is it!

The man – it was definitely a man – stopped outside the door. He waited for a second, his hand perhaps on the handle, then he turned and went into the room next to mine.

I breathed out hard, almost sobbing with relief. I had been momentarily spared my discovery. I had sunk to my knees. I reached up to steady myself on the handle of the door. My hand felt something else instead, and I flinched it away.

There was a rattle, a faint rattle. I had inadvertently knocked something that was hanging off the wall. I'd made a noise; not much of a noise, but out of place in a vacant room. I put my hands up to steady its swing, and when I did so I knew what I was touching: manacles and rope and chains; that's what I had bumped into.

They were here. It had been real. This wasn't a

made-up thing. My hands closed around the bracelets that had locked that woman's arms. She had worn them, been strung up in them, while the author had taken her manfully. I must be kneeling where her feet had been as he had posed her for her thrashing. She had stood where I was, unable to get away, gagged with her own lace panties. They would have been moist from her own juices, dripping with her shame. I knew her desire, for I felt the same, the longing to be taken. My envy returned once again. He had seized her and tied her and whipped her and fucked her, all in this very room. I pressed myself, despite myself, and then found the door handle to escape.

Please don't hear. Please don't hear.

I begged the fates he had not heard the disturbance. I eased the handle, achingly slowly, so as not to squeak the hinges. The coast was clear – or so I thought.

The light went on in the room. I spun around. He was standing behind me, looking at me, from a second door to an adjoining room.

"Who are you? What are you doing here? You little thief! Get the hell out my place!"

I ran, I sprinted. I took the stairs two at a time. I could hear him now, right behind me, his feet pounding like galloping hooves. I fell on the first landing. I always fall. I started to crawl away.

"What do we have here?"

I crawled, frantic, on hand and knee. He took a sore grip of my dark curled hair just as I'd reached the

31

next set of stairs.

"Oh, sir. Please, sir, no!" I pleaded, but he put his hand on my mouth to stop me. I bit hard on his fingers only to find he'd gagged me …

"Jesus Christ! You bit me."

There was no leather gauntlet. Somehow I'd thought … He pulled his hand from his mouth. I could see his fingers were bleeding.

"No, no. Please." I fought him. He pinned me down and forced my arms behind my back.

"What are you? Some junkie thief? Breaking into houses." He was on top of me now, pinning me down, but then his hard voice suddenly changed. "Wait a minute." He pushed my hair aside so he could see the side of my face. "I know you. I know who you are. You're that girl from across the street."

He let me go. I don't know what was worse. Being caught for a thief or recognized. He knew me!

"You care to explain yourself, young lady?" He wrapped his hand in a handkerchief and then helped me to get up. "Are you hurt? A fellow might have killed someone they found sneaking around their house."

"I'm okay." In truth, I was a little winded and my scalp was sore where he'd pulled my hair. I became weak recalling his formidable strength as he had pinned me to the floor. His body had been as hard as iron pressing against my own.

"Just you rest a second. I can fetch you a glass of water. Jeez, you bite like a crocodile. And what are you doing here?"

"I'm Paula," I said sheepishly.

I'm not normally a weak girl, but his presence and the embarrassment of being caught sneaking into his house made me want to curl up and disappear.

"I know who you are, Paula. Mrs. Miller gave away your name. But tell me why I shouldn't call the police or hand you over to your Aunt Em."

"Oh, don't do that!" I was sincerely worried. How could I explain this to her?

"No? You don't want that? Well, you're a curious thing. First peeking through windows and now breaking in."

I must have blushed.

"You've got a very pretty colour to your face when you blush. Are you sure that I didn't hurt you?" He ran the back of his finger across my cheek bone, and something in me melted.

"Not for saying? Okay. Well, maybe you're shaken. I tell you what. I'll offer you a deal, but if you don't take it I'm handing you in."

"What is it?" I was so naïve.

"I'm going to take you out to dinner. I'm going to pick you up tomorrow at eight."

"Eight?"

"That's right. We'll go somewhere nice. You can tell me all about this then. But if you say no or if you stand me up, I'm setting the dogs out on you." He had an irrepressible smile.

I was almost out the door, ready to flee, when I

remembered the letter. I dug in my bag for a couple of seconds then thrust the envelope into his hand. "Here," I said. My face must have been scarlet. I turned from my captor and ran.

AND THAT'S HOW I MET Max Broekner, a pen name for many dark things. That's how I landed my first date with him, which was the start of everything else.

CHAPTER 4
A DATE WITH DESTINY

I HADN'T BEEN ON A DATE IN … I forget. High school, of course, and the first year in college – I was a busy girl then – but after my sophomore year I was pretty much going steady. Way back. Too long maybe. Obviously, I guess. My guts were turning, but it wasn't out of fear that Max would turn me in. That's not why I was nervous. If I'm honest it was something else. It wasn't even my wardrobe, though that was a problem to fix. I was going on a date that evening, somewhere nice even, and I didn't have a thing to wear. Most of my stuff was still in the city, and though I love Aunt Em, "farmer's wife" was not the look I was hoping to make. I was going to have to do my best.

I lucked out in one of those discount stores that sells the designer stuff the big stores can't shift. I tried not to think of how many women had passed on the wrap dress before it ended up in my hands. I liked it, though. In fact it was perfect. It hugged me through my chest and waist and was loose down to my knees. It was short-sleeved with a splash of cleavage and was open at the neck. Not too much, but enough. I was old enough already to know my charms and wise enough not to oversell them. With that dress I could get away without a jacket and the purse I had would match. I considered my flats, but I scored a pair of new pumps that I knew would show my legs well. They were a little high for my regular tastes, but I didn't want to look frumpy. I picked up fresh nylons; I don't often wear them, but I had a bruise come up on one knee. I bought a new lipstick, too. If there was going to be any kissing going on, it wouldn't be in Aunt Em's Avon chapstick. I came home from the stores very pleased.

"You look cheery. Going out tonight?" Aunty Em's radar was on.

"I've got a date, actually. Sorry, I won't be home for dinner. I'm being picked up at eight."

"Anyone I know?"

"That author man, actually, from across the street. I met him returning a letter."

"Reeeeeeallllly," she drawled. Her eyebrows were up in her hair.

After I showered I put on scent. I don't normally wear perfume, but tonight I felt I was somebody different. I was turning a page. I put a dab on my wrist, then rubbed it on my neck; then, after a thought, smeared a little behind my knees and between my legs and breasts. *Paula, you slut*, I told myself. *What are you getting yourself into?* It might have been too much, it *was* too much – Aunty Em would never approve.

I picked out my silver choker necklace, a present for a birthday. It was a solid band that fit snug and tight around the middle of my neck – did it look a little bit like a collar? I remembered the book in Mr. Broekner's study. I wondered if he'd notice such things.

He was right on time. I'd been standing in the hall for ten minutes.

"Hello."

"Hi."

"You look great."

"Thanks."

"I'm glad you decided to come."

"I'm glad you asked. Beats the hell out of the police station."

He held the car door for me and closed it when I got in. I couldn't help thinking that the gesture was a little old-fashioned, but I liked it all the same. It was sort of like him: a little bit older, a little bit wiser, a little bit more mature. Confidence and manners. I felt like I was a lady. The car must have cost a bundle; no one I knew drove something like this. He got in.

"I like ethnic food. There's a new Indian restaurant that's getting rave reviews. A bit upmarket: discreet tables, bright white linen and dark wood furniture, high ceilings with slow fans that hint of the heat of the subcontinent. That's what the web page said, anyhow." There it was again, that irrepressible smile that he seemed to wear with everything. His tussled hair never seemed to sit, but the rest of him was very clean cut. He wore an indigo jacket, the colour of a Van Gogh starry night, and distressed dark jeans that looked good on him. He had a collared shirt and chisel toe leather shoes that looked casual but smart at the same time. He wore no jewelry that I could see and his skin had been out in the sun. He slid prescription glasses over the hint of sideburns as he put the stick-shift into first gear.

"I can crash just fine without them, but they come in handy for reading street signs."

I'd left my own glasses back in my room. I had been too self-conscious to bring them.

"They suit you."

"You think?"

"They make you look smarter."

"Smarter than what? No ... don't say."

We talked and laughed about little things. The journey wasn't a long one.

"Sure it is," he replied to my question; I couldn't believe that was really his name. "But with a name like Maximilian Broekner, I either had to be an evil industrialist or become an author instead."

I've always liked men that can make fun of themselves. There's a confidence that gets me.

"Half the world thinks Max is a made-up name, and who am I to correct them?"

He was a gentleman. He wasn't lewd or pawing, but I thought I caught his eyes, once or twice, glancing at my body. That was okay. I wanted him to look. I managed to wriggle my hem a few inches higher and give him a glimpse of my thigh. The upholstery was leather. Although the weather was perfectly fine, I noticed the seat heater was on.

He had made a reservation. There was no burn to the fare, no heat, but it was spiced and flavoured to entice the taste buds without overpowering and numbing the sensation. The naan breads were warm and fresh; the basmati rice had a hint of saffron, which left a slight stain wherever it fell off the plate. I had a glass or two of wine, the only thing not authentic on the menu. Max refused the eggplant: "We are enemies until the grave."

The tablecloth was long, I remember that. At some point our knees touched under the table. We continued to talk and laugh.

"So what kind of books do you write, Max?"

"You mean you haven't looked me up yet?"

I must have blushed and given myself away.

"Mysteries not your thing? That's okay, they pay the bills and I like what I do. Not many men get to say that and mean it."

"I'll read yours, I promise."

"Well, maybe you will, at that. So now you know that I do for a living, but that puts me at a disadvantage. What brings you back to Grand Falls? My sources tell me you went away to college. Did you get homesick all of a sudden?"

My heart skipped a beat. He'd been checking up on me too. "Well, there was a guy … "

"Oh, oh. Watch out for those. He's not here, I gather? Either that or your Aunt Em has him locked up in her basement."

"No. He's not around anymore. That's over."

I told him it all. I hadn't told anyone. Aunt Em I'd spared the details. Somehow I needed to get it out, and he was good at listening.

"You know, somewhere in the 'First Date Manual' there's a chapter about not mentioning old boyfriends."

"Oh, Max, I'm so sorry."

"No, no. Don't you worry one bit. I think you're very brave for what you did."

"Really? You do?"

"Can't have been easy. I don't as a rule pass comment on relationships, but that man of yours sounds like an idiot."

"He was an idiot."

"There you go then."

My cheeks were burning. I'd a smile stamped on my face that I couldn't shake for trying. He stretched out a hand and covered my own. Part of me felt like crying.

"So, what were you doing in my house yesterday? I think there's a story in there."

I had known it was coming, but that didn't make it easier.

"I was ... " Would he really tell Aunt Em? Would he enforce his deal to the letter?

"You were what? Snooping? What were you

hoping to find? You weren't after money, so what brought you into my house?"

I felt like a little girl. Caught, being bad, and forced to tell. I might have rubbed my knees together. I must have looked deeply ashamed.

"I wanted to see." I barely heard the words myself.

"What did you want to see?" He was unforgiving.

"The place. That room." I couldn't make the words come out of me.

"You wanted to see the room where you spied on me with those women?"

I nodded, eyes down. Ashamed of myself and embarrassed at the topic and horrified that he spoke so openly of it.

"And what did you see, Paula? Tell me. Tell me exactly what you were peeking at."

"The women. They were … they were tied up."

"Yes, they were."

" … and you were hitting them."

"Disciplining them – a subtle distinction, but an important one."

"They were tied up and helpless, and you took them."

"And do you think they were happy or unhappy? Do you think they were enjoying it?"

"They were tied up," I said again, defensively.

"But do you think I kidnapped them? Do you think I dragged them up there? Do you think what happened was entirely against their will?" He had been in a very serious frame before, but something in this last part amused him.

It seemed a very important point, and I tried to remember what I'd seen. Had they seemed unwilling? No. They hadn't. The women had obeyed at a whispered word; the ropes were put on later.

"Why were you watching, Paula?" He leaned close into me now. He gave my fingers a gentle squeeze to calm the trembling nerves. "Why did you spy? Why were you looking? Why did you break into my home?"

"I was returning a letter … ," I whispered breathlessly, his lips very near to my ear. He seemed to be inhaling the scent from my neck. His head moved closer to me. Then I felt his hand, his hand on my leg, pressing gently on top of my knee. I may have flinched; it was an electric shock, but he didn't take it away.

"I don't think you were." His words rolled like gravel. His hand on my leg made the tiniest of circles. My loins ached warm and wet. "I don't think you were returning a letter. I don't think you stayed up all those nights looking out for the mailman."

I couldn't answer. I waited breathless, immobile.

"I think there was something that you saw that touched a secret part of you."

How could he know?

"I think there are rooms in your intelligent mind that even scare yourself. Maybe you don't admit they exist; I'm certain you don't tell others. Are these lustful places? Are they dark places, Paula? Do things happen to you in that part of your mind that you don't admit to or share with others?" His hand was moving, but only a fraction, up the inside of my leg. The thought didn't occur to push him away; I felt my knees open instead.

"Yes, I thought so," he said, one hand covering mine, the other brushing my nylons. "Is that why you came over that day? You had to see it for yourself?"

I couldn't answer. What girl could? How could I tell him it wasn't the place, it was him I needed to get close to? He was excited and pleased, I could sense it. I caught a glimpse of his lap and a telltale bulge betrayed what I knew already. I wanted him then. I'd wanted him before, but at that moment I would have let him take me on the table. If he'd pushed me over and fucked me there I couldn't have been any happier. But he was too experienced for that. I realize now he was reeling me in, that I was already hooked and caught.

He took hold of my hand and moved it to my lap, replacing it for his own. He spread his fingers on top of mine and pressed my palm between my legs.

"Please, Max."

The waiter was coming by infrequently now; we were settled, and aside from one table in front of ours we had our privacy from the room. I felt my own hand being slowly guided, being pushed over my leg, stroking my thigh. My own hand caressing me, the sensation of muscle in my toned leg, the smooth glide of the denier nylon, the soft swirls of my own finger tips.

"Touch yourself," he whispered it in my ear. He released me, leaving my hand in place. "Put your hand between your legs and touch yourself while I watch you."

It was dreadful and it was blissful. I felt the eyes of the room upon me, though there was only one table nearby. My skirts had been pushed and my trembling fingers fluttered on top of my groin. It wasn't just my own stimulation that aroused me. Max hovered over me like a bird of prey, his carnal desire for me radiating. He wanted me. He needed it. He was almost not in control of himself. I had never experienced the desire of another so tangible and life-affirming. He wanted me, and this desire for me was a stimulant that fired my own. I surrendered to his command – it was an easy choice – I touched myself a little.

"Good girl," he said, his eyes were on me, feasting on my mouth and breasts. I could feel my areola tightening up, my nipples pressing hard to my dress. His hand once again was on my leg, stroking me as I touched myself. I pressed and rubbed at my arousal through the nylon of my hose. I could feel a dampness with my fingers as I touched my intimate bud.

I was breathing hard. "Please, Max, there's a couple right there."

They were sitting not eight feet away. He was checking a Blackberry. She, pretty and obviously bored, was luckily looking away. I was close. My fingers relentless and steady.

"Open your legs, my sweet. Do as you are told."

It was shameless, but I was helpless. He pulled suggestively on the inside of my leg and I spread my knees wider in reply. My skirt was in my lap, my thighs exposed. Max looking down on me as I obeyed. For the second time he put his hand over mine and pressed me to myself.

"You like it, don't you." It wasn't a question. He was close to me. My leg moved over his knee.

The woman at the table turned towards us, drawn by something she couldn't quite place. She stared openly for a couple of seconds, confused about what she was seeing. I dropped my eyes and fought to forget her; my excitement was swelling in strength. I closed my eyes and lent into my hand that Max pressed against the mound of my sex. The sensation on my clitoris, firmly touched, was fired by even the slightest of movements. I shifted my weight and bit on my lip. I was close – I was grinding my palm.

"Look at you. Such a bad girl, rubbing yourself in a restaurant." He pulled my hand away and I am ashamed to say I resisted. "Leave yourself alone, you dirty girl," he admonished me, and held my wrist tightly. "Sit still. You are not allowed any more for now."

He made me put both hands on the table after

rearranging my skirt for me. He kept a protective hand clamped on them both so that I couldn't move them away. Held like that, I let him spoon-feed me gulab jamun, Indian dessert, warm and sticky and sweet. My nipples stuck out tautly. I was forced to squirm without release, loving every moment.

Max was paying. There was no splitting the bill. It didn't seem appropriate to argue. I went to the bathroom to arrange myself as Max settled things with the waiter. The woman from the other table was gone, although I noticed her husband was still texting. The washroom door narrowly missed me as it opened for a lady leaving.

Inside, I went to the vanity where I was standing when the air drier cut out. The noise of it was soon replaced by a most curious revealing sound. There were three stalls, but only the centre one was closed. It was obvious to me that the occupant thought she had the privacy of the room. Perhaps she was sitting, straining to hear the outside door in case it opened, but she had missed me coming in. Whoever it was, she was clearly amusing herself.

I stood frozen, eyes on the mirror, catching a shadow move between the crack around the closed stall door of the cubicle. From within came noises of arousal: strained panting and gasping and rubbing sounds trickled into my ears. I was already damp from Max's handling, and her masturbation aroused me. I grazed my nipples with silent fingers in an empathy of lust. She was near, very near, yes, do it, girl, yes … oh oh! Such a gasp! Such decadent release. I envied her the pleasure. Who had she been thinking about when the moment came?

I stood still as a statue as the door to the cubicle opened. The woman from the table froze in shock as she locked eyes with mine through the mirror. I turned the tap on and the hot water rushed. My eyes dropped to save us both the embarrassment. I saw her legs pause in the mirror – strappy high sandals and bright red painted toenails.

She stepped forward and washed her hands while I pretended to do the same.

"You're very lucky." I scarcely heard her words. She dried her hands and left.

I stayed another minute, collecting my thoughts, my body awash in forbidden sensations. The couple was gone when I came out. Max was holding my scarf.

"Everything all right?" he asked. Of course it was. I was on a date with him.

He drove me home. There was a stretch of silence, then:

"I don't want you to crease your dress. Pull your skirt up, Paula."

"What do you mean, Max?"

"At the back, pull it up. Do it now."

What could I do? He was so direct.

So commanding. It felt like an order. It would be starting a fight to say no, but in any case I didn't want to refuse. I wanted to let go. I couldn't speak, but I did as I was told. I had to squirm in the seat to work the material free, pulling it higher as I did so. He could see me. He was watching me, not hiding it. I felt on display He was looking directly at my thighs and hips, uncovered and sheer, black and glossy from my new pair of pantyhose that covered my backside and belly.

"Now slide your nylons off, down over your thighs. Put your bare skin against the car. Arrange yourself with propriety."

He was smiling. Enjoying himself watching me struggle. It was difficult to do what he asked with the seatbelt on, but I managed. I wondered how this looked to the passing cars, but I did it anyway. I wanted to please him. I wanted him to be happy. I wanted his approval of me. It surprised me how eager I was to win it, but then I was still near the edge from earlier. I got the nylons under my ass and felt my bare skin against the leather.

"Tidy your dress, Paula. Smooth it out so nothing appears out of place. Make it look as if everything is normal. I want you to look like a lady."

What did he mean, look like a lady? It was he that told me to take off my hose. I did as I was told, and I found that I enjoyed it, the sensation of being naked and hidden. I hadn't worn underwear – I didn't want to show a line. The heated leather warmed my skin. It was novel and not in the least unpleasant, more so for being under the direction of the handsome man beside me. The car stopped at a light.

A truck pulled level. I could feel the eyes of the driver looking down on me. Could he tell how the power of the engine pressed intimately against me? Was something in the way I looked giving me away? The light changed and we drove on. I wanted Max to take me.

I wanted him to take me home and drag me on his bed. I wanted him to tie my wrists and spread me on his bed frame. I wanted him to blindfold me and force my legs wide open. I wanted his teeth on my breast; I wanted his mouth on my ass and between my legs. I wanted to feel the sting of his belt and be forced to take him into my mouth. I wanted these things and couldn't ask, but my body begged him anyway. He reached over and stroked the side of my face, the outside of my eye and my cheekbone, then he slipped that hand inside my dress and cupped my breast and held it. I did nothing to stop him. I felt safe and protected. He took it away and placed it on my knee and left it there like a mark of ownership.

He didn't take me to his place. He pulled up in front of Aunt Em's.

"I've had a very pleasant evening, Paula. Thank you again for coming. But I think you need to make an honest decision before things progress any further."

I wasn't sure what he was saying.

"Go home. Go back to your room, and take off your dress and look at yourself. Lie on your bed and put your hand between your legs and finish with what you are needing. When you come, I want you to be honest with yourself. I want you to ask yourself what sort of woman you are. What kind of girl you are choosing to be. What do you want out of life. Because if you come into my house again, you won't be permitted those choices. The next time I find you upstairs in that room there will be no backing out. There will be no more decisions. I will make them for you.

"Go home and think about it. Walk away now, if you choose; but if you stay there will be no leaving."

Then he kissed me. Our first kiss. Tender and longing. And he saw me to the door before leaving.

I did as he bade me and looked hard at myself, naked under the mirror. I snuck into bed and spread my legs and cradled my breasts as I masturbated. It was the Colonel again, but it wasn't him, for this time he had unruly dark hair. And he hunted me down through the forest in the park but caught me as I ran up the stairs. He bound me to the railing, and pushed me face down, and threw my dress over my head. My pantyhose were pulled off my ass and he whipped me with a switch till I screamed. I cried and writhed and fingered myself, feeling the bite of every swing. Then he unbuttoned himself and withdrew his ardour that was firm with the lustful heat.

I didn't know what Max had meant when he talked about making decisions. I didn't know what he was hinting at when he said *if you stay there will be no leaving*. I didn't understand then. Not like I do now.

The waves of release surged through my womb as I worked fingers through my petals to my orgasm. My only thought was to be taken by him and made to serve his will.

And so, in my way, I had decided.

PART 2:
SURRENDER

CHAPTER 5
THE LOVERS

I WAS ILL WITH INDECISION. My date with Mr. Broekner had left me in a state. I was sick with worry that he didn't like me and I'd never see him again. He hadn't called. It had been two days.

"What's the matter with you, girl? You haven't touched a thing on your plate." My Aunt Emily was clearing the table. She didn't approve of good food going to waste. But she wasn't cross; she cared more about the funk I was in. Having looked after me for years as I grew up, she had more than my appetite on her mind. "Paula, my dear, don't be down. If he's right for you, you'll know it."

It embarrassed me that she'd noticed; but why hadn't he been in touch? Didn't he like me anymore? I remembered the touch of his hand on my skin and his lingering goodnight kiss. I'd thought that he wanted me. I knew that he did. Then why had I gone two nights now without even hearing a word?

"I just thought he'd call, Em. I thought he liked me, that's all."

"He likes you just fine, or else he's a fool not worth knowing. Life's too short to go chewing yourself up, imagining made-up slights. Search your heart, girl. You follow it. Now you best eat that good fish or else you'll end up blind."

I gave her another two forkfuls, and then I excused myself from the table and returned to my reading in the front room. My chair was by the window. It looked out over the park. I could just see the outline of 88 Vale Street peeking through the trees on the far side. 88 Vale Street, where Max Broekner lived. I hadn't turned a page in hours.

Was he playing games with me? Was he waiting for me to call? *An honest decision.* That's what he'd told me to make when he'd left me at my front door. *What kind of girl are you choosing to be?* He'd told me to think about that. What kind of a question was that, anyway? What kind of man said that? Then he'd made me touch myself. Well, that wasn't strictly true – he'd asked me to. And I had. I had slipped into bed as quick as I could and put my hands upon myself. And I'd loved it. Thinking of him. Thinking of him touching me. I liked doing what he told me – his little orders masked as requests – and with each one I wanted more.

If you come into my house again, you won't be permitted those choices. I remembered his words very clearly. I wondered. Was that an invitation he'd extended?

I had been cast adrift from his mysterious life; there would be no phone call to invite me back. If I wanted Max Broekner and all of his secrets, I had to find my own way in. Going over was my answer. It came to me sitting there. That was what he meant. *Walk away now, if you choose, but if you stay there is no leaving.* I made my decision, perhaps the last he'd allow me: I chose to pay my author a visit.

IT WAS A LITTLE AFTER LUNCH. Enough time to put on my best jeans, sort my hair, and fight for ten minutes with my makeup. The angel in me wanted nothing at all, the whore in me begged for mascara. I ended up with just a little lip gloss – I didn't want to appear too eager. I thought I looked fresh. Fresh was surely good. I pinched my cheeks to give them colour, then worried that I looked out of breath. It would have to do. I was as ready as I was going to be, and I still had no idea what I'd say.

A short, wiry lady answered the door. She rather startled me. I hadn't expected anyone but him; somehow I'd thought he lived alone. I hadn't seen anyone coming or going. She was old and kind looking, like a shrunken Aunty Em. She looked like one of Santa's elves, cheerful and slightly unreal.

"Yes?" the lady inquired. She rolled out the word like a welcoming mat, with a smile that stretched to her wrinkles around her eyes. My fears were put at ease and I found the courage to stay and ask.

"Ahhh … I'm looking for Max, please? I thought, perhaps, he was in?"

"You must be Paula, then?" She looked me up and down, as if approving of what she saw. "I'm his housekeeper, Mrs. Andrews. Pleased to meet you. Come in. Mr. Broekner is working in his study upstairs; he told me to send you up if you came."

My first thought, when I'd seen her, was that I was looking at Max's mother. I felt immediately friendly towards Mrs. Andrews just because she wasn't.

"Follow me, please." She held the door open for me. "I'll show you the way."

I couldn't tell her I'd been there already, though there was a gaiety about her that made me wonder if she knew of my earlier escapade. We passed the clock and mounted the stairs, and she paused in front of his closed-door study. She gave a deferential knock and waited for an answer. I could hear the chatter of a typewriter stop.

"Enter."

The word came short and clear. Mrs. Andrews showed me in.

"A Miss Paula for you, sir."

He was seated behind a walnut desk, with his bookcases framing him. In front of him was a manual typewriter with paper wilting from it – an Apple computer sat to the side, deferring to the more ancient technology. Mr. Broekner did not rise.

"Thank you, Mrs. Andrews. That will be all for now. Hello, Paula. Thank you for coming. You look very pretty today. Please come in and stand on the carpet. I will be with you in a moment."

Mrs. Andrews closed the door and left me alone with Max. It was a strange request – *stand on the carpet* – but there was nowhere obvious to sit. He seemed engrossed in whatever he was doing and went immediately back to work. He wore a button-up collared black shirt, open at the neck and rolled up at the sleeves. His head hunched down between broad shoulders, and his fingers struck the metal keys savagely. *Snap snap snap. Snap snap snap.* The carriage juddered along with his sentences. A tiny bell preceded an instinctive swipe that returned the page to a fresh beginning. They made a great deal of energetic clatter. I didn't want to disturb.

I didn't know what to do. He was immersed in his work, and it seemed rude to interrupt him. His concentration on the page was so complete that I got to worrying that he'd forgotten me. And what was I going to say? *Can I stop you for a second, Max? I just dropped by to say hello, and I was wondering if you liked me?* I felt silly now, like a foolish girl. Why had I done this? It was so embarrassing, and yet it felt so good to see him. This was where he worked – this was him creating. He was inventing and molding characters and breathing life into them as he typed them. There was something very appealing in that. He was in control, making plans for their lives, deciding what happened to them. It was strange, but already I felt a part of his world, as if I was closer to him.

From the moment I'd decided to knock at his

door, my tummy had been turning butterflies. I started to feel more comfortable now, waiting for him on his carpet. Hadn't Mrs. Andrews expected me? Maximilian didn't seem surprised that I had come. That meant he hadn't forgotten me. Perhaps he'd been thinking of me as well. *Snap snap snap. Snap snap snap.* What was going on behind those eyes? *Snap snap snap. Snap snap snap.* He typed like the beat of a drum. When it stopped, it was as sudden as it had started. He looked up. Stared right at me. I knew then what a deer must feel in the presence of a hungry big cat.

"You have come." He was smiling and I must have smiled back. Everything was well.

"I have," I said redundantly.

"That is good. I am very pleased." He got up out of his chair.

I hadn't moved from the rug where Mrs. Andrews had left me. He moved unhesitatingly around his desk and walked steadily over to me. He seized me. He took me firmly in his arms and pressed his body to mine. The first time we had kissed, I was wearing heels and had only to tilt up to his lips. Now he gripped me in powerful arms and almost lifted me from my feet. I leaned into him and closed my eyes, offering my tongue to his. But what he did next surprised me greatly and took my breath clear away.

He gripped my wrist and led me forward, his other hand in the small of my back. He guided me to the edge of his desk, and then stopped me two feet away.

"Lean over it." His voice was clear, presumptive. I heard the gravel in it, the way he'd talked to me in the car, the tone that spoke of a pent-up passion. I hesitated to obey, and in that next second he pushed down on my neck. He was strong. It didn't hurt, but I could not resist him and found my face pressed against his desk. My breasts rubbed against the edge. He put his free hand upon my hip.

What was happening? Oh, my goodness; his hand fumbled at my belt. I made to shift but he pressed down harder, holding me in place.

"Max ... " He had my belt undone. He unzipped my fly. He started to push the hips of my jeans down over my thighs.

"Max ... " Hushed words of what? Objection? Desire? He didn't answer in words. I reached behind me and he seized my wrist and held it behind my back.

"Oh!" I gasped.

He pulled my other arm around beside it. He had my arms locked at the elbow and I couldn't move or turn. Though I couldn't see them, it felt as if my jeans were now at my knees. I felt helplessly exposed. And wet.

"What did you think about on the night I dropped you home? On that night when you touched yourself?" He pushed his hand between my legs and rubbed me through my panties. My white cotton bikini briefs were pressed into me by his persistent touching. His strong fingers, firm from pushing keys, wrote words of desire on my labia. Lust. Hunger. Need.

"What were you wanting when you touched yourself?" I grew swollen and wet as he spoke to me. He fingered me roughly through the material and I writhed against his attentions.

"Did you want a man to lie between your legs?" He held me, pinned down over his desk, my legs trapped by my jeans that had fallen past my knees. "Why did you come back here, you dirty slut? Did your pussy make you do it? Did it cry out for a real man's cock? Is that what you want to fill you?" He was crude and carnal. As rough with his tongue as he was with his fingers whose touch I was squirming against. "Are you here because your pussy told you? Are you a slave to this thing of yours?" He hooked a finger under the elastic and worked a finger inside my panties. He ran it through the slick folds of my mound before searching deeper inside me. I pushed down against him – I couldn't speak – I responded without choice.

He withdrew his hand. I was shaking and sobbing. I missed his touch already. He pushed those fingers inside my mouth before I knew what he was doing. I almost gagged. I could taste and smell the slickness on them that had come from my own desire. Why was he doing this? Was he trying to shame me? I could feel his hardness against my leg.

He slipped my own belt from its hoops bound my forearms together. I felt the buckle bite as he pulled it tight – I was trapped and tied and his.

He was taking me. He was having me. He had expected me and I had come. *There will be no more decisions … I will make them all.* Is this what he meant? But what if I didn't want his attentions? What if I screamed out for Mrs. Andrews? What if I wasn't willing to be undone, bent over his desk for his pleasure? Yet I could not shout out; though I had not said yes, still I had come back to his house willingly. He was no longer offering me any choices – he was taking from me what he wanted. I felt the excitement in his assumption, the affirmation that he desired me.

He wet his fingers on the insides of my mouth, scraping the insides of my cheek. He took them out, dripping saliva, and put them once again between my legs. This time he didn't stroke my lips or my bud, he thrust them inside me instead.

Oh, dear lord! I may have moaned. I hadn't been touched by a man in a spell. Even when I had, it had been fumbling and nervous, but Max forced me with a confidence I cherished.

"That's it, you little whore. You like it hard and rough. I bet you dreamt of a big hard cock spreading you wide and opening you." He fingered me, two possessive fingers inside me, thrusting into me as he spoke. "I bet you thought of being chased and held down, or being tied to the bed and taken. Slut. That's what you are." I had never been called bad names, sexual names, and the shame of it aroused me disturbingly.

"Cock whore. You little slut. You want it, don't you? You want it. Your pussy's begging for a real man's cock to take you and use you like you want."

God yes, I wanted it. How did he know? I felt like the slut that he called me. He was undoing his own pants. I couldn't see, but I could hear him. I wanted to be taken and used. I wanted to be filled and joined with a man who was strong enough for the both of us.

I clenched my hand, his fingers entwined with my own, as he continued to push me down. I turned my face, still pressed to the desk, so I could look at his beautiful face. I could see the taut muscles on his tanned forearm working to loosen his belt. I missed his rough fingers inside my sex as he used them to free himself.

He lifted his cock out and laid it on my back. I groaned in anticipation. He lifted it and brought it round and touched it between my legs. I shook with a carnal longing as he teased me with his firmness. His forehead pressed my cotton-clothed mound and I moaned in the passion of my distress. He pushed his cock head over my pubis, running it back and forth. He pressed his teeth into my shoulder as he worked in a teasing rhythm.

"Max. Max … ," I gasped. He peeled my panties to the side so that my labia were exposed. Into my lips he touched his erection, which was warm and rigid and solid.

"Oh! Ohhhhh." I yowled like a cat in heat as he

nudged my clitoris with his man's root. He must have been holding his cock at its base and directing it onto my pearl. It was really happening – I wasn't being asked – I was being taken just like I wanted. I was going to be mounted here in his office, and all I could think was "yes."

"You want it, don't you, you dirty girl? You want to spread your legs wide and take it." He taunted me with it, his own hardness swelling as he glided it over my clitoris. "You come to my house with your pussy all slick. You have given me your decision."

I didn't think much about what he meant, for at that moment he lowered his aim. He skillfully found my eager channel that led into my womb. He held himself there for a second. I tensed. I held my breath. I could feel his forehead flared and thick, poised with elemental purpose. Slowly slowly, he edged himself in, spreading me wide as he pushed me. An inch, another – oh, the girth! I hadn't felt such a heat in years.

I raised my hips to coax him. He held his cock head inside my entrance, not moving for a few seconds. He shifted his touch so that I could feel him move; then he withdrew and brought it back out. I cried out in despair, emitting a shameful longing. I needed the touch he had promised me. It was cruel to deny me it now.

"You want it, don't you? Say it." He pressed his manhood again to my folds. "Say the words, you dirty girl. Let me know the kind of woman you are. Let me hear those words."

"Yes," I whispered. "I want it." He was making me speak my desire.

"You're a dirty slut, Paula. Say it out loud. You're a greedy, cock-loving Jezebel."

"Yes," I whispered. "I am what you say. I'm a dirty girl. I am."

I was a cock slut. He was making me say it. I'd never said any such thing in my life. I felt like a dirty girl to say these things, and yet it felt oh so good. I now wiggled my ass, hoping to tempt him. I wanted his fat cock more than anything. He'd made me say it, I didn't have to pretend. He knew me for what I was.

He knew it.

"Ohhhh!" I gasped as he slipped fully inside me, thrusting his full length through my channel. He didn't stop till he pressed my womb; I felt his weighty balls slap at my petals.

Now it was his turn to gasp. Max, my lover, filling me completely, the ardour I'd felt from him realized. He wanted me. He needed me. I clenched myself around him. I felt him tight against my walls and I squeezed down on him with my muscles.

He began to stroke inside me. Small thrusts then steadily larger as his passion built inside me. My initial tightness against his substantial girth now warmed and loosened to take him. *He. Was. Fucking. Me. Hard.* He pushed deeper into me. His thighs slapped against my bare legs with the violence of his passion. I groaned as I was driven forward, and I felt the desk judder beneath me. My breasts were pinched the edge, squeezed not unpleasantly. He swapped the hand that was holding my wrists and took hold of my hair.

"Ah!" I cried out again. It was sore, his tightening grip pulling at my scalp, forcing my head off the desk. He held my hair like the reins of a horse and drove me again and again. Faster now, faster faster – he stroked into me from behind. His breath became harder, he was working a lather, he wouldn't last much longer. I stood on the tips of my toes to receive him as he rutted me like an animal.

I wanted to touch myself. I wanted my hand, or his, on my special place. I was very near but I was not there yet when he bucked and shot inside me. I could feel him shudder and the heat of his seed as it spilled uncontained inside me. He slowed his pace. I wanted more. I craved his cock to finish me. It wasn't to be. I wanted him to pin me down and fuck me hard till I screamed. I wanted him to tear my clothes and whip me with his belt. It was not to be, not this first day; he grew softer and slower then stopped. He leaned over me, his body on mine, keeping himself in my chamber. He rested his lips against my neck a little back from my ear. He pushed my hair gently aside. I could hear his softening breath.

"Good girl." Whispered praise. He stroked the side of my face. After soft moments together, silent and close, he finally slipped out of me. I felt myself run with his sticky gift, the evidence of his need. He wiped himself with a paper tissue which he left in a ball on his desk. "Pull up your panties and jeans."

He told me to go home and come back the next day. He told me to come at ten. He kissed me then, and sent me out, and I obeyed his wish. I knew in my heart I had done the right thing. I was starting to learn his ways.

CHAPTER 6
HIS WAYS

PUNCTUALLY, AT TEN A.M., MRS. ANDREWS admitted me to his study. Max wore a white shirt today. It looked good on him; trim and fitted, the sleeves rolled back, as was his habit, the neck open as before. He wore button-fly jeans. I noticed. He sat on the edge of his desk. The room was the same as yesterday but for a chair in the middle of the carpet. It sat empty, expectant.

"Thank you, Mrs. Andrews. That will be all." She closed the door behind her. "Please take a seat, Paula."

I did.

There was a moment of awkwardness as I straightened my dress and sat attendant with my hands together. I felt a bit like a schoolgirl looking up at the handsome young teacher. "I hope I'm not interrupting your writing." I kept my knees pressed tightly together.

He seemed amused. He seemed to find the

humour in almost anything.

"You most certainly are, young lady. But I'll let you off this time." The only lines in his face were those from laughter. He would be handsome when he was old. "I'm going to show you a couple of things. I want you to learn why they are important."

Was it going to be a class after all? Was I expected to take notes or something?

"I'm going to blindfold you." My heart started pounding immediately. "Sit still."

I could hear my quickening breath. The day before, when I had returned home, I had lain on my bed for hours. I had submerged myself into the sensation of him that felt like bruising on the inside of my legs. I had smelt his body on me, his juices inside of me. I had ached to come but had in the end resisted, knowing I was seeing him today. To say that I approached the chair already wound up was an understatement of great order. I had touched myself as I had showered and dressed; I was aching for a renewal of his affections. And now he was going to blindfold me. What did he mean to do?

Would he leave me? The fear of that stuck like a lump in my throat, but I used logic to swallow it down. Why would he ask me to come and then leave me? I had to give my self over to trust. He would be in control. I would have to let myself go.

He took a scarf from a desk – not a man's scarf, I thought, and I wondered at that for a moment. It was black and transparent, though when he folded it over it became entirely opaque. There was no scent on it and it was not wrinkled. I had the feeling that it was new.

"Sit up straight. Look straight ahead. Don't move your head an inch." When he tied it around me, I was immediately plunged into the sooty blackness of imagination. I was alive with anticipation to whatever he might do next.

I could smell him. Shaving soap and mint toothpaste and a hint of fresh wood shavings. Why wood shavings? Why that?

"I am blindfolding you for two reasons, Paula."

His mouth was close to my ear. I had worn my hair coiled and up, clasped in place with an Asian pin. A pleasant shiver spilled down my back from the warmth of his breath on my neck.

"The first reason I am blindfolding you is because I want you to be aware of your body. By having your sight taken away, you will become much more alert to sensation. All the sensations of your body." He ran his fingertips over my shoulders.

Even Max talking about my body brought a tingling flush to my skin. I felt goose bumps rise on my flesh. I could feel my nipples grow taut and ripen. I wondered if he was watching this and if they showed through the hug of my dress.

"One can rely too much on the eyes. I want you to be keenly aware of all your senses."

I couldn't see him. I couldn't even peek through the bottom of the blindfold. I had lost sight of his face, but I could picture him clearly still – his kind eyes and the strong defined chin. And I felt him. Not just his hands, his fingertips now tracing their way off my shoulders and down the length of my arms; I felt his presence as a dark mass too, a gravity close behind me. The weight of his masculine frame bearing down over mine. His trim waist and broad shoulders, the muscles of his thighs. Perhaps he had been chopping wood? That would explain his scent. It was an earthy perfume that suited him well in this room with its stale smell of books. Taste alone I did not have, but I knew what my tongue and lips craved.

"I want you to feel your body and be aware of it always, Paula. Your body is alive to sensation. If you are open to sensation and welcome it always, it can be a source of much heightened pleasure."

He was still standing behind me, but now his arms came around to enclose me. I felt his hands graze my chest and tug at the buttons of my dress.

"Another thing I want you to learn is trust." I felt him unbutton my top. "Don't move your hands," he ordered. I held onto the seat of my chair. My dress was tugged, this way and that; I felt the air brush the top of my chest. "Yes, very pretty indeed." I keenly felt my vulnerability, conferred by the blindfold I wore, but I surrendered to him as he unlaced me and made pleasant with my chest. I did not object or struggle.

I had worn my lacy white brassiere that pushed me up in a balcony cut. I had never been happy with my chest; I was a terrible envier of other women. My nipples seemed far too big for my breasts, and any cleavage was a hypothetical achievement. When I was young I was ashamed of my breasts; I used to hide them from the girls in the changing rooms. Giving them to him, as I did now, was a far greater trust than he knew. Yet he liked them, he called them pretty, and gave them affirming attention.

His hands, course-skinned hands grown rough from chopping wood, perhaps, slid around me and lifted my breasts. His fingers pushed inside my brassiere and pulled me from my cups. I writhed. I pressed my chest up and away from the chair, striving to meet his touch. My hands gripped tightly onto the seat, and I squirmed my ass against it. His thumbs hooked under my nipples and dragged them back and forth. My mouth opened wide, my lips glossed with saliva from my excitable tongue.

"Exquisite, Paula. That's what you are."

He gripped them. He pinched my bosom, then I felt his mouth close tightly around my nipple. He suckled it hard and pulled on it sorely – he pressed it with strong white teeth. I didn't see it coming: He took away his mouth and then slapped my breast, which made me cry out in shock. Immediately, his mouth was upon me again, suckling the soreness till it was gone. He kissed the tender heat raised on my breast by the strike of his hand. He tugged on my nipples and pulled them with wet fingers and rolled them with his thumbs.

"Oh, oh," was all I could manage. It hurt, but it felt so good. Having his hands on me and the caress of his mouth without even being able to see it. I knew I was grinding my ass on the chair; I wanted the release that I'd missed. I cradled his head as his mouth latched onto my nipple. I pushed my fingers through his unruly hair.

He stopped.

"You were told to keep your hands down." He stood up.

"Oh, Max … " I knew. I hadn't meant it.

"Stand up, Paula." I struggled to my feet. My balance was off in the blindfold.

He handled me. Man-handled me. He sat down and pulled me to him, bending me over his knee. Before I knew what was happening I was draped over his lap. I could feel the bulge of him pressed against me as the back of my legs were turned up.

"It looks like there is to be another lesson today, young lady. Sensation. Trust. And now rules. When I tell you to do something, you will obey – or there will be consequences. This is not a relationship of equals."

Not a relationship of equals. I was beginning to understand. I squirmed and kicked my heels in desperation, but it was all to no avail.

"That's very good. I like a little fire. It makes your bottom look even more tempting and sexier, if that were possible." Just as yesterday, he pulled my hands behind my back and I felt him draw my dress up my legs.

"Max, no, Max!" I thought I understood what he intended. Then just as I'd feared, he began to spank me, his open palm stinging the flesh of my rear. "Oh, oh!" I shrieked. It stung me cruelly, the shock as much as the pain. He slapped one cheek and then the other, each spank sharper than the one that preceded it.

"Max, please!" I begged him; it was warm and sore, the rhythm of it forming a pattern. I fought the terrible embarrassment of being handled this way, the squirming shame of being spanked like a child. A grown woman over the lap of a man? It was too humiliating to bear. Yet I could not get away. He had my arms, he held my wrists, and I could not free them to fight it. His legs were at a height that I could not slide off his knee and my feet were barely touching the floor.

Down came his hand, chastising me, and then I had to admit that his forceful discipline was arousing in a terrible way. It mixed with my frustrated helplessness and warmed me shamefully. I was wet! He was spanking me and it was sore and sharp, and my soreness was turning me on. It wasn't the pain – oh, please make him stop! – it was being under the power of this man. He did with me as he wanted and I had no strength to resist. I could feel his hardness pressed against me as I flexed with each new blow. Oh, please make him stop, I'd do anything for him. Let me sit down on his cock.

"You will say 'sir.' You will say 'Please, sir, I have

been a bad girl.' Say it, or I won't stop."

It was so demeaning!

The next few were much harder than the rest.

"Oh oh oh!" He was proving his point. He could make me do anything he wished. "Please, sir! Please, sir. Please. I have been a bad girl. Please stop. I'll do anything."

It didn't feel strange or odd. It felt of nothing but relief. He desisted his caresses immediately. My bottom flushed hot and sore. I couldn't see a thing – my blindfold had stayed tight – and my breasts hung free and exposed.

"Kneel on the floor, you disobedient girl. Lean over the chair and be still."

I obeyed him this time without waiting. I felt him throw my dress over my back and then he bent his mouth to my backside. He was tending to me. Soft strokes and gentle kisses across my buttocks and flanks. He was ladling them out on my sore skin just as he'd done when he'd slapped my breasts. He was soothing my heat with his tender affections when his fingers brushed between my legs. I moaned at this touch. It came from deep within me, a noise of relief and pleasure. His fingers strayed again, perhaps less incongruously this time, running over my ridges. He removed my panties without ceremony. He pulled them off over my knees. I was conscious of all of my physical senses, and again they all said "yes." He stepped away but was then soon back. I heard a noise of something plugged in.

"This will be your final lesson today, Paula." He put his hand assertively over my pussy and held my mons protectively. "What is this I've got?" he asked me.

"My pussy, sir."

"It is no longer you that owns this pussy." He put a finger inside me. I bucked. "It is no longer you that owns this pussy. This pussy now belongs to me."

Did I blush? I could not say. I was in no position to know my feelings beyond the gut-wrenching lust of being claimed. Here I was, spanked, undressed, bent over, blindfolded, and with his finger inside of me. Here was my lover, telling me I was owned, claiming my sex for his own.

"It is mine. Do you understand me? I tell you when you are allowed to come, and I decide when it is forbidden. You may touch yourself in your private moments, but you may not release without my blessing. Is that understood?"

I did not speak. I could not. He spanked me hard and furiously.

"Oh, sir! Oh, sir!" I begged him off, his hand still on his property. "My pussy is yours. It's yours to own. I'll do whatever you want of me."

"Yes, it is. It is mine." He let me be. He stroked my hair, caressed my breast, ran his palm down over my backside. "Now, Paula, you will come. I am going to see that you do. You will release because you're a dirty girl who loves doing just what she's told."

He turned it on; I could hear it then, the thing he

had plugged into the wall. I knew the sound before he even touched me with it: a vibrating wand. He was direct. He didn't tease. He pressed the massager between my legs and ground it into my mons. Oh lord, how I trembled. I bucked and swayed. I fought to get it off, for its attentions were so alarming, and yet I could not for he followed my lead.

"Oh sir, sir!" It was an intense purr, a cat's tongue without let up or relief. I had been aroused when I'd arrived, and then turned on by being blindfolded, and his breast play had made me run wet. His disciplined hand that had spanked me sore only served to make me grind hot on his knee. And now, here, on my knees before him, with my dress thrown over my back, here he was taking the last resistance from me; here he was proving his point.

He moved, but the wand rode me still. I felt his hand in my hair tighten, lifting my chin once again. Then I found his cock touching my mouth, nudging the side of my cheek. I obeyed. I knew. I wanted it too. He didn't have to tell me. I took his half-soft, growing erection and sucked him to make him full firm.

I trembled. My thighs shook without hope of control. Electric waves of pleasure radiated, spreading out from my core. I fought for my breath, choking on his girth, as the first waves of my release spilled over me. I saw rainbow light behind my blindfold and thrashed to escape the vibrator, but its continued attentions on my poor battered clitoris were an unbearable pleasure to take. On and on, he forced it on me while I gagged on him in my mouth. My orgasm drew out till I nearly wept, and then I collapsed, curled up.

He turned off the vibrator. "Very good girl." He bent down to pet me. He lifted me up and sat me on his knee, kissing the side of my eyes and my temples. I was weak. A puppet in his arms. "And what did you learn today? You, perhaps, are a little more appreciative of your senses, and aware of your vulnerability. You've learned the basics of trust and of rules. And whose pussy is this?" He laid his hand between my lap.

"It is your pussy, sir." I had no resistance left. He left his hand there possessively.

"That's right, Paula, it belongs to me. And when are you allowed to come?"

"Only when you let me." The thought excited me still.

"That's right. Very good. That's enough for one day." He removed my blindfold. "Better that you go home now. I will see you here tomorrow at eleven."

The sudden light was painful; I had to blink my eyes at first. "Eleven, sir?"

"That's right."

He kept my panties; he didn't say why. Mrs. Andrews saw me out. I walked back through the park without underwear. I felt like the village hussy. I wondered if anyone looking at me could tell what I had been up to.

Aunt Em saw me come in. I went straight up to my room. I inspected my backside in the mirror – it was blushing, but nothing looked permanent. I bathed in warm water with salts. I was hot inside and out. I had a bruise on my breast that looked like a bite. The slick flower between my legs looked foreign to me now. I felt enslaved by it – a joyous, wanton enslavement – and yet it was itself now owned by another. What had I gone and gotten myself into? It was still too tender to touch.

I knew my pussy – Max's pussy – would call on me very soon, and would I be able to resist it? Would I be able to stop myself from going where it led me? And did I even want to? I slid my head beneath the water and reveled in my submersion.

CHAPTER 7
RITUALS

AT ELEVEN IN THE MORNING I presented myself just as Max had requested; or instructed, rather. Mrs. Andrews once more let me in and efficiently escorted me to the study. All had the semblance of normality … well, normal for that house and its occupant. I could hear Max writing. I knew by now that this was his habit from eight until lunch. Lunch he took at one.

"I've been with Mr. Broekner for over ten years. He never allows disturbances to his writing routine."

But I was an interruption. I took from Mrs. Andrews the gravitas of that. "Then why did he tell me to come at this time? I might have come in the afternoon."

"Why indeed?" Her eyebrows lifted. "Clearly he's quite taken with you. Whatever his reasons, I'm none the wiser. You don't want to be late." She knocked, and as before, Max summoned us to enter.

"Very good, Mrs. Andrews. Hello, Paula. Mrs.

Andrews, please take Paula downstairs with you. You will show her how to make tea."

Mrs. Andrews tried to cover her surprise. "Very good, sir. As you wish."

Mrs. Andrews pushed me back out. The noise of the typewriter resumed.

"What does that mean?" I asked as soon as we were a little bit away. I was a little distraught. I felt he had sent me away.

"It's been many years since anyone has been allowed to fetch him his tea but myself. You should be careful, my girl. He's clearly fond of you."

I wondered at what she could mean. The implication was that there had been others, but some time ago. A long time ago? *Many years.* What did that mean? And not for the first time it re-entered my mind that I'd seen Max with those other women. Truth was, I had never shaken them from my thoughts. The picture of them being taken.

I knew I had been at fault, at first, spying on a private man. What business had it been of mine who he loved or how he went about it? What did I care? But that had changed. It had changed when he had captured me and made me go with him to dinner. It had changed when we had talked that night and I'd gotten to know more about him. He had grown from a shadow in a dimly lit room to a man I had strong feelings for. I could not keep those feelings straight; I wasn't sure what was happening with us. One moment I felt only lust; I would believe that this was nothing more than a fling. I was making up for the affection I'd been missing in the cold years of my old relationship. But those thoughts only lasted a second. I couldn't deny that this was becoming more, that it was the man, and not just the passion, that I was being drawn towards.

He was a chimera, my Mr. Broekner. He was exotic, but also an ancient ideal – a dark man who shaped his own destiny and didn't always follow the rules. While others slaved away at the nine to five, he carved success from his own brains and his efforts. While other men's lives were sport stats and TV, Max lived life to the fullest. He set his own rules within his beautiful house, and lived for the moment and deeply. I could not deny the appeal. He succeeded in the contrast. Bold and reckless, safe and successful, he blended them and excited me. Back in college I'd had crushes on the occasional young Professor. It was always the same: He was a little older than me, smart, confident, and expert. I was drawn to capable men, strong men. Men that could take care of me and yet challenge me to grow and be successful. Men like that I felt in my head and in my heart and lower. For men such as that I wanted to prove myself and secretly give myself over.

I felt this from Max. Max had that charm, and yet he had something more besides. There was, upstairs, the attic room – the ropes and manacles and the chains. Max wore a cloak of shadows through which I glimpsed a sensual world. It was a dark world of unbidden pleasure that I was reluctant to acknowledge existed. Reluctant because of my own desires that were tempted by their promise. Reluctant, too, because of those women, the other women I had seen him with. Max had never talked about them, and I could not bring myself to ask him.

I had never seen them again. I ached to know just who they were and what he felt for them. But why should I care? We had only just met. Yet deep inside me, I did care. I wanted to know what they meant to him, and by extension, what I meant as well.

"This is the tea tray." Mrs. Andrews had me in the kitchen. "He takes it at around eleven, not before, and no later than a quarter after. The pot must be heated first."

Mrs. Andrews poured hot clean water into the waiting steel teapot to illustrate her method. The container would not have looked out of place on a frontiersman's smoky campfire.

"The water must be boiling hot when added to the leaves – not just sort of hot, boiling; do you hear? That bit is very important." She turned on the switch once again to a recently steaming kettle. "Fill it to here. That's his cup. Bring the milk in a jug separately. No sugar."

"That's it?"

"Up you go. Six years since the last girl I remember was allowed to bring him his tea. Six years. You seem like a very nice girl, Paula. Be careful not to spill anything."

I STOOD HOLDING THE TRAY in the middle of the carpet. His hand was upon my leg.

"Look straight ahead."

My hands trembled a little. I could see ripples on the milk jug. I tensed my body to hold myself straight.

He was close behind me, almost spooning me, his hand flat on the outside of my thigh. His fingers inched my hemline up, to the flesh at the top of my stocking.

I wanted him, his hand on my puss – his pussy, since he had claimed it. I wanted him to bend me over the desk and take me like the first day. I wanted him to lay me down on the floor and to feel his weight upon me. I felt his animal arousal swelling up behind me – I remembered the taste of it in my mouth. His hand reached the black mesh of my panties – I'd worn my skimpiest pair. I could smell the tea, the acrid black leaves stewing, and I fought to control the rattle of the cup.

"Whose pussy is this?" he whispered though my hair.

"Your pussy, sir." I gave my hushed answer. It was true enough what I spoke.

His confident fingers rested over my smooth folds. I had shaved myself that morning.

"Good girl. Now pour the tea, and bring it to my desk."

I was writhing, but I controlled myself and did just as he asked. He watched me as I poured for him and presented him with his cup. He sipped from it. Very hot. He held the cup rim gingerly so as not to burn. He looked me over.

The weather in Grand Falls had turned to cold, as it did this time of year. I had worn a black woolen skirt and thigh high socks, which stopped my boots from rubbing. I had felt the need for my turtleneck sweater, which if not entirely sexy at least showed the shape of my chest. Aunt Em's house was draftier and colder than Max's insulated rooms.

"Thank you for my tea."

"You're welcome."

"It's perfect."

"Mrs. Andrews showed me."

"I meant everything."

I blushed a little. I thought it was perfect too.

"Are you happy here, Paula?"

What did he mean? "Of course I am." Perhaps I sounded a little concerned.

"I just mean that things are not moving too fast. I don't want you to be scared."

I wasn't scared at all. I didn't know exactly where things were going, but I was safe and content and happy. In truth, since my talk with Aunt Em three days before, I had lived in a cocoon of bliss. I had never met a man who I could be myself with, who I didn't have to explain things to. I didn't have to pretend with Max, he was just … stable, accepting … intense.

"Where are things going … sir … if you don't

mind me asking?" I was trepidatious, nervous at what he might say. He lingered a while over his tea, then put the cup back on the desk.

"I like you very much, Paula. I like you being close to me. In fact, I think you ground me. I feel complete when you are around, and that is very special for me. It has been quite a long time since I could say that, so I want to move things between us slowly."

I *grounded* him! I melted inside with joy. I made him feel *complete*.

"Yet I do want to move things a little. I want to start you with a couple of rituals that will gauge how receptive you are."

Rituals? Whatever might he mean?

"Tea is one of them. I am a little old-fashioned, I'm afraid. I happen to think consistency and order bring stability and peace to one's life."

Part of me agreed. I made him feel *very special*. I'd have agreed with whatever he said.

"So it is that when you are available, you will now bring me my tea. Do you understand?"

"I do."

"Very good, Paula."

He wanted me every day!

"There are other rituals too. Come here."

He made me come around the desk until I stood at the side of his chair.

"One of these rituals I am going to call 'Inspection.' Do you know what that means?" He put his hand on my leg once again. I could feel my heart beat faster and my breath began to come quick.

"No, sir. I don't." But I was guessing.

His hand ran down my leg to the top of my boot then up the inside of my knee. He spread his other hand over my ass and held me as he stroked me.

"It means that every day that I see you, I will inspect you for what you wear. I will lift your dress or open your shirt and inspect your body and underwear." He was liberal and certain with his touch, reaching up my thigh. His left hand slid from over my ass to my belly and up to my waiting chest.

"Lift your sweater."

I obeyed. I wore a lacy mesh bra that went with my panties; it opened at the front. He stroked my chest, then held my skirt and lifted it up to expose me. I stood before him, my socks stopping at my thighs, my pussy looking towards him.

"Yes, lovely." He kissed my mound, then pressed my hips with his hands and turned me to face the wall. "Put your hands on the bookcase and lean over. Open your legs a little."

What was he going to do?

"If I am going to have you, Paula, I'm going to take all of you. If we are going to be together, there will be nothing we do not share."

All of me. Yes, sir.

I cast over my shoulder and saw him sit with his finger in his mouth. He dipped it in his tea to heat it up and then he touched it to my ass.

I squirmed.

"Still, my girl. Stand still. Has no man ever touched you there? Have you never had your dirty place taken?"

The Colonel would sometimes put a finger there as he drove me from behind, and I would sometimes dream of being locked away with two men at the same time. I would be pulled onto the one, kneeling over him, so that my bottom was raised off the bed, and in my fantasy the other would join us and couple me from behind. Moving back and forth, off one cock and onto another, my belly swollen with the firmness of both of them inside of me. I had dreamed it but never done it – I had touched myself there, was all.

Max was not a dream. His wet warm finger circled my sphincter, the wide pad of his fingertip and the hard flat short-trimmed nail. He leaned forward and nudged my tightness with the tip of his tongue. I felt the flicker of pleasant pressure back there that sought to open me up. Again his finger, circling and touching, pressing me gently and persistently. Then, wet from his mouth, he touched me firmly and I felt myself give. I opened to him and he pressed his way in. His finger invaded me to the knuckle. I whimpered as he moved it around while my muscle gripped him tightly.

"That's it. How does that feel? How does it feel when I take it out?" He did so and the sensation of closure was both dirty and provocatively arousing. He was playing with my ass. I was being invaded! A shameful, filthy taboo.

Oh, Max! What had he made me do? He had made me stand up against the bookcase. He had uncovered my ass while I watched. He had made me stick my ass out for him and spread my legs to open. He had touched me in that secret place and put a finger inside of my hole. It was so private and intimate and filthy to like it. I felt slightly shamed by it all.

"I'm going to have you. I'm going to fuck you there, once I've trained you to take me. Would you like to feel my cock in your ass?"

"Oh, sir!" He was going to train me.

"Yes, Paula. You're going to be my ass whore. And not just there. You're going to take me in every part of your body. I'm going to fuck your mouth and your tits as well, and also your ass and cunny."

"Sir!" He'd put his finger back in me after making it wet with his saliva. It was easier to open up this time. It was like squatting on a shower when he opened me up – that momentary shudder of intense sensation followed by a pleasant pressure. I felt full, and the tugging arousal built from knowing I was doing something sordid.

"Tea is a ritual. Inspection is a ritual. And so is training your ass." Without letting go of the finger he had in me he opened his second top drawer with the other hand. I could see something in it. It was in a box, newly delivered from a courier. He lifted the top and brought the glittering metal weight out.

It was smooth and heavy and solid-looking. Tapered, with a bulb on one end. I was not so innocent that I didn't know what he had – he'd bought an ass plug with a flared jeweled end. He held me. He made me stand, posed, while he lowered it into his tea. He kept the toy in the warming cup before licking the steel of it clean. He smothered it in a film of saliva before bringing it to my ass. He withdrew his finger but before I closed, I felt the pressing warmth of the toy. It was bigger, wider than his forefinger, but it was smooth and solidly persistent. I gripped the shelf with both hands and gasped as he widened me with its touch. A little push. A little more. He moved it gently, persistently, but further in each time. He backed it out till I was almost closed and then pressed me again with its wedge.

I was scared. Scared I would evacuate myself. Scared that I'd shame myself in front of him. Scared that I couldn't take it. He had moved one hand over my puss while spreading my ass with his other. He tongued me a little, making it slick, and gradually won me over. I felt huge for a moment, distressed that I couldn't take it, and then suddenly it was in me.

My stretched ass closed snug and tight around the narrow neck. Inside my back channel the steel plug nestled, while the jeweled base held the toy in place. He kissed me there.

"Touch it," he told me with pride, still with a hand on my puss.

I reached back around and felt the ridge of the jewel nestled between my cheeks. It had been ruby red, and I imagined it sparkling as Max spread my buttocks to watch me. I could feel its weight, like a warm round stone, filling my ass from the inside. Even as I moved I was conscious of being touched in that most private of places. Max set my panties back over it and covered it up with the mesh. He squeezed my ass and gave it a kiss to show his approval of me.

"Very good, Paula, that is perfect. You may take it out an hour after you get home. You will wear it inside of you every day this week. You will carry it for no less than an hour each time. You will practice putting it in and taking it out. It may feel strange at first to wear it, but you will grow very comfortable with it."

Already I felt an urgent stirring from the size of it and the weight. I tightened my Kegels and was conscious of the pressure it exerted on me back there.

"I have your puss and now your ass. You can see we are making progress."

He let my skirt drop. He hadn't given me permission to touch myself. I was aware that I was the same girl that had walked in, but somehow I was also much different. I carried his toy inside of me. There was a weight in my ass that was him.

"Remove your sweater. Fold it properly. Put it on the desk. Very good. Now unclip your brassiere – I like the style, by the way – and put it on top of the pile. Put your hands at your sides; don't cover your breasts. Your body is mine to admire. Yes, my dear, you are beautiful. You are a wonderful, attractive woman. Now stand up straight and lift your hair off your neck. Lift both your arms up clear. That's right."

I did everything he told me. When he was satisfied he withdrew from the same second drawer a long, smooth black rope. I couldn't exactly determine its length, but it may have been twelve feet or so. In diameter it was the width of my little finger. He folded it in half to find its mid point, and then, perhaps eighteen inches down, he folded it to create a knot. Into this loop he put my head, which cause me a little fright.

"Don't fear, my dear Paula. I would never hurt you, unless you needed it or for fun. This is a ritual I'm going to call Binding. I will show you it now. I'm going to weave you a special harness to remind you how close you are to me. It's going to grip you safe and tight, so there will be no forgetting."

He was very clever with his hands; sometimes it was hard to follow him. He measured the rope to beneath my breasts where he put in a second knot. The spare line draped over me to the floor for a second before he gathered it up.. He now wrapped this, delicately, precisely, firmly around me, circling it behind my back. He drew each line beneath my breasts and then threaded it through the circle of rope he'd formed between the two knots. Back once more, behind my back and then out in front of me again, but above my bosom. As he tied it off, I could see the effect: my breasts were pinched between the rope strands. I was held, girded in a brassiere of rope that fastened around my neck. I could move and breathe without any restriction, but I was tied tightly and bound nonetheless. My breasts were stimulated, pressed gently and yet exposed. I felt like a slave girl or a risqué vaudeville star. I felt secure and yet on display. He was the first man who had ever tied me up, though this was really more like dressing me. I was later to learn this was called *shibari* and had a lot of curious uses.

Max wiped his thumbs over my nipples, forcing them to rise. He kissed me gently on the mouth and then told me to get dressed. I had to leave my bra behind.

"That is enough for one day. Gather the tray up and take the tea things downstairs, and then tell Mrs. Andrews you are leaving."

I knew then that he meant to send me out wearing the things he'd put on me. I was to carry the ass plug inside my body and wear the rope breast-harness under my sweater.

"There's a mirror in the hall." He seemed to read my mind. Sure enough, with the turtleneck, no one could see the rope lines. I was the same girl in her boots, high socks, and black skirt, holding her handbag. Except I wasn't. I was part of Max's plans – I was learning his rituals: the serving of tea, the daily Inspection, the training of my ass. The Binding. What had he said? I made him *complete*? He was a glove to my small hand.

"How long must I wear it for, sir?"

"You may remove it before bed. There are no knots except at the front. You uncoil it from the back, then unwrap it. You may take it off earlier if it gives you pain or if anything starts to feel numb."

Half a day for my breast-harness. One hour for my butt-plug. I was sent away a happy girl with orders to return.

THAT EVENING I LAY ADRIFT near sleep, in that land between worlds of reality. I had been nabbed by Aunt Em just before lunch and recruited to accompany her for groceries. It had been a surreal experience, walking with Em, pushing that trolley up and down aisles, saying hello to everyone. It was tedious enduring the gossip of neighbours, being judged by them under their stares. "You've come back, eh, Paula?" a dough-headed high school dating experiment had greeted me in the dairy section. I made a mental note never to come near again.

But the oddest thing was they hadn't seen me; they didn't know who I was. I would smile and nod, but underneath I was bound tightly in Max's black rope. And beneath my skirt, under my damp mesh panties, I carried his ass toy within me. I was being trained; I could only guess for what, but I wanted it heart and soul. They didn't know me. But he did.

I HAVE OFTEN SINCE WONDERED whether what happened the following day was as unplanned as it first appeared to me, or whether Maximilian, the consummate plot weaver, had arranged the disruption himself.

It went like this ... but that is for another story – the start of the end of my tale. Tonight, outside, the wind shakes the window, and I must off to sleep. That tale must rest awhile, and still it seems a dream.

PART 3:
SUBMISSION

CHAPTER 8
DOUBTS

I'VE BEEN KEEPING A DIARY since I was little. I found an old one of mine in a dusty box that my Aunt Emily had kept aside – an old diary from high school and a couple of curios in a dry musty shoebox. That in itself was odd. Aunt Em isn't usually the collecting type. She looks like she is – don't all old people? – but normally she couldn't care less. Em lets things blow through her fingers; she doesn't put value in possessions. Em always says it's people that matter: your family and friends and relationships. She's the sort that gives stuff away – she keeps the Goodwill store in business – but something had made her hold onto this box, and she'd done it thinking of me.

"Would you look at these! When did you set all this aside? What were you thinking, Em?" I'd found the shoebox out on my bed; its lid was brittle and as dry as old leather. I opened the box carefully – one corner was split – and I examined the treasures within.

There wasn't much order or sense to it, unless you were measuring sentiment: my grade nine photograph showing me posed, shoulder dipped, with the world's worst faked up smile. I had to laugh at what I was wearing. I'd had a fight with my mother about wearing that dress, since I normally wore nothing but jeans. I remember that I'd lost the fight that morning; they must have heard us down the street. But twenty years on, I had to admit my mother had got it right. I was prettier than I remembered.

"You kept my retainer, Em?"

"It never hurts to have a spare."

"That is totally gross." I moved the offending article that had tortured me for years gingerly to one side.

There was a bow from my ponytail, still in a knot. It wasn't one of those fake pre-tied ones. My mother could weave elaborate loops that looked like tropical butterflies – the sort you see in those TV shows when they talk about the Amazon. I stopped wearing bows in high school. It hadn't seemed cool anymore. I wondered if I would ever have a daughter so I could weave things into her hair.

Then there was my journal.

It was an old assignment book from back in the depths of grade nine – I laughed at the drawings in the margins. "Who the heck was Scott Parker?" I asked. I'd gone way overboard with the love hearts.

"Parker? Wasn't he that tall boy? Real tall? The

one with the curly blond hair?"

"Oh, my God, Em! Yes, he was! How do you remember?"

"You and your sister and the rest of your gang were crazy for any fool throwing a ball."

That wasn't strictly true. It wasn't strictly untrue, either.

"But what's with the box? Why'd you keep it?" There was a report card, and a couple of pictures. There was one of me and Em's old dog, a big slobby brute called Chew.

"Oh, I have my reasons." Em stroked my hair. "I'm allowed to get old and sentimental. Put it all back when you're done. I was just thinking of you, Paula: why you are here, how long you'll stay, and what you will do when you're gone. Just crazy old Aunt thoughts, is all. It made me remember this box here of yours. I knew it was somewhere abouts."

I was sitting cross-legged, the contents of the box spread all about. It is humbling when someone cares for you, and everything here showed it. I guess I was too silent; she was fishing for answers, and maybe she was a little concerned.

"You stay as long as you like, girl. We can go get your stuff from the city, or I can call that ex-boyfriend of yours and get the damned fool to send it out. There's no rush to do anything. No need to rush anything at all. I think you know what we're talking about. Well, I've got dinner to start thinking of."

Em left me with my box. The first half of grade

ten had seemed very complicated at the time. I leafed through the diary on the bed and gave thought to what Em meant.

Maximilian Broekner. That was who we were talking about. My author 'friend' from across the street, whom I'd only met a week before. Or was it longer? Do I count the time I was spying on him from my window across the park? No need to rush anything at all.

Why had I come back to Grand Falls? To get away from the city? To get away from my dead-end relationship, for sure. But was everything that had happened to me just moving a little too fast?

I blushed. Oh God! If Aunt Em knew the half of it! What had I let myself into? Was she suggesting I was a little bit vulnerable and getting into something too quickly? I had to admit that Max and me had 'rebound' written all over it.

I had wanted to have a career, get married, and have some children. I'd wanted to be that girl in the magazine photos that made everything look easy. But how many years do you let things drift before you figure out the passion is gone? He was never going to ask the question; and if he had, what were the odds that our sex life would have gotten any better? *Paula, girl, how can you be so smart in the head and still so dumb at heart?*

Coming back to Grand Falls had been smart. Falling hard for Mr. Broekner? The jury was still out on that.

Whenever I thought of Maximilian Broekner I started to uncoil, like there was a worm twisting deep in my belly that stroked me from inside. Okay, maybe not my belly. Maybe a little lower than that. He wasn't an infatuation like Scotty Parker, too many love hearts and exclamation marks and nothing else going on. No. He wasn't that. Max wasn't an infatuation; Max was a shameful urge. A need? Maybe. But was it *him*, or just a stage I was going through after being held back for too long?

At first, I hadn't even known his name. He was a shadow behind a window. The man in black across the street, a dark figure laying claim to a tied woman. I so wanted to be her, to trade places with her. I wanted to feel the possessive hand of his desire on me. Was that wrong? What woman would say otherwise? It was by sheer accident that I'd seen him; I can't be blamed for that.

Then I kept watch. Was that innocent fun? I was curious; but really, who wouldn't be? And he was more handsome than I'd imagined. Not in a film star or oily way, but in his strength and independence and honesty. Okay, maybe now I was embellishing, but a girl gets stirred up, and he had a nice ass – no one could deny that. And hair. *Oh, Paula!*

But wasn't this going to happen to the first guy I met? Wasn't this just the classic rebound? Was this not what Em was warning me about with her blunt hints about taking my time? The first real man I came across – what were the odds that I would lose my head? It hadn't helped that Max carried an aura of mystery, and that his vices ran to the dark side. How could Em – how could anyone, even me – have known that I'd meet a stranger who could compete with the Colonel?

The Colonel is my shadow world. My hidden self. My secret. I've read enough self-help columns to know fantasies aren't wrong. Hell, I got a 95% on my first year Psychology exam; I could even teach the subject! I'm a career woman. A feminist. A believer in women's equality, in both principle and practice, and I'd kick any man in the balls that said or told me otherwise. Yet I know there is a part of me, of my sexuality, that hungers for a powerful man. A man who can protect me. A man who can take me and make me his. A man who would pursue me and seize me, who would want me enough that he would stop at nothing to have me. I like to feel desired – is that wrong? A man who would take what he wanted from me and I would know his strength and passion. The Colonel did that, does that for me. The Colonel knows my secret. And he makes me admit that I want it too, which doubles my shameful desire. There is something erotic in the very shame of it. I would be his if he ever claimed me.

I caught myself just in time.

My eyes were closed and I had touched my breast, just as my fingers reached down to my panties. Maximilian!

Whose pussy is this?

It is your pussy, sir.

You will not touch it without my permission.

Oh, dear lord! I stretched my fingers wide and stroked around my legs, circling that which I may not have. It was a new torment, this one – the torment of denial. Knowing I was not allowed to touch it made me want it even more. I was claimed. Why did I find that so hot?

But how stupid was this? Why couldn't I do anything that I wanted? Really, what was going on with me and Max? What did he mean to me?

I wanted him. Yes. There was no doubt of that. I tracked him down into his house. I'd felt compelled to see what sort of man it was who lived such a mysterious life. The books in his study and the old typewriter and the tropical plants in the atrium – they were a hint to the man he was, and still there was the room upstairs. That room upstairs where he did those things I had only dreamt about. *Okay, Paula, you silly girl. You probably gave it away when he caught you.* Why had I admitted to seeing him upstairs when he was with those women? What kind of girl gets turned on from that? What kind of girl goes peeking? He probably thought I was a slutty whore. How could he ever respect me?

But isn't there a little bit of slut in you, Paula? Well, isn't there? Be honest. Don't you want it?

I blush a little in confession. But I'm a nice girl too. I am. I'm a real woman. I'm complicated. So?

What of it? And hadn't Max been a gentleman when he took me out and insisted on buying me dinner? He could have been a complete asshole. He could have been lewd or slimy or demanding. But he wasn't.

But you wanted him, Paula, didn't you? You'd have let him take what he wanted. You might have protested otherwise, but in your heart you wanted him to drag you inside and force himself upon you.

Yes, I wanted him. It had all happened so fast. I was caught up in the heat I'd been missing. I had wanted it, but he hadn't taken advantage; he had given me a choice instead: *Your last decision.*

IT WAS GOING ON TEN-THIRTY. What was I going to do? Max had told me to be over at eleven, and I'd need from now until then to get ready. But was I going to go? It was obvious to Aunt Em that I was infatuated with my new friend, our author neighbour from across the road. I'm sure she was happy for me for 'getting out there' and starting to meet anyone new. But she really didn't know. She didn't know, she would never know, the bond that had started between us.

I'd gone over and Mrs. Andrews had let me in and brought me to stand on Max's carpet. It was as if I had presented myself; I can't pretend it wasn't exciting. It was a blend of embarrassment and exposure and desire – wishing for him to accept me. And he had. Oh, more than that. He had made me lean over his table. Not asked. Not requested.

Ordered me to bend over his bureau where he had slaked himself in my body. *Hands on the desk. Do not move.* He had lifted my hips and made me stick out my ass and he had unbuttoned my jeans and removed them. He had entered me freely. *Oh, Paula!* I could feel the ghost of his presence in me still. The firm girth of his ardour parting my petals and filling my channel with man. A real man. I had glowed afterwards. Lovemaking before Max had been fumbling and gentle, but with him it was confident and hard. He was assertive, firm, even rough. I responded as I'd only imagined before when the Colonel had hunted me down. I gave myself over to Max. He had claimed me and held me and filled me with his seed, and then he had sent me back home, warm and blushing.

And I had wanted more.

The next day I had returned to 88 Vale Street, as per Max's instructions. Where was the doubt on that second day? Indeed, there had been none. I had bathed and perfumed and even shaved myself, leaving most of me smooth to the touch. I had gone with lacy panties – ephemeral and tight – knowingly trying to lure him. *Bad Paula!* But I had wanted more. I had wanted all that he would give me. I'd even worn a dress instead of my usual jeans to tempt him with a look at my legs. Hadn't I been trying to encourage him?

Then why was I doubting myself now?

Max had accepted my offer. But it had been

different from what I'd expected. I was still trying to figure it out. I had dreamt that he would meet me and kiss me and lead me upstairs by the hand. But he didn't. He hadn't done that. Not then. It was clear I still had much to learn. *Sit in the chair, Paula. You look very pretty today.* Why did his compliments make me light up? I hadn't been told I was pretty in years. He made me feel like a little girl – well, not that little. One solitary chair in the middle of the carpet; how I had squirmed against the wooden seat!

Max had used a blindfold on me. He took his time putting it on. There was a helplessness, a drop in my stomach, when the world around me went dark. And then my senses went into overdrive. Every fingertip, every bit of skin became hyper-sensitive to touch and sensation. My smelling and hearing became alert to each of his commands and movements. The warmth from his breath. The smell of wood shavings. I ached to reach out, to touch him or myself, and satiate the desires that were stirring. But he had given me an instruction – *Do not move your hands!* – and I had disobeyed.

Never before had I known a man who extracted punishment for such transgressions. Rules were rules with him, though, and I had been taught to obey – it was a lesson I wouldn't forget soon. He turned me over and pulled me onto his lap, handling me like a toy doll. I felt his hand raise my skirt and expose my backside to the room. And then he was spanking my ass.

I squirmed now, reliving the torment, the shameful burn of desire. I had never before felt so helpless and yet aroused at the same time. He was hard underneath me, his bulge a firm ridge, and I slid over it as I writhed against him. I had started to count his smacks but I lost track of the number, and I was burning when he steadied his hand. What must Mrs. Andrews have thought downstairs! *Paula, hang your head, girl.* I blushed to remember my cries.

He had taken my panties and sent me away after claiming my pussy for his own. The presumption of the man! The cheek of it all! Yet I had accepted his word as he pronounced it. I walked back through the park with the shame of my nakedness hidden under my skirt. But I knew what he had done. And had I touched myself that night? *No, Paula, girl, you did not.* I had lain awake dripping lust from his assumption — Max's pussy indeed.

IT WAS TWENTY TO ELEVEN. I was going to be late. What was I going to do? Were things moving too fast? Was this what I wanted? What did I really know? What, if anything, was Max about? Did he care for me at all? And did I care if he didn't? Oh, it was all getting so mixed up!

The day before had been the worst, or the best, of everything so far. He had given me the hour of my appointment — summoned me — and I was growing used to being obedient. *Rituals.* That's what he'd said. That's what he talked about. He was grooming me for something. Preparing me. Testing me. Those words excited me yet scared me at the same time.

He's never let anyone bring him his tea for more years than I can remember. Was Mrs. Andrews on my side? Was she suggesting that Max really liked me? I thought so.

Small rituals.

Little services.

Being of use and desired by somebody. I couldn't help but like the notion.

Yet I couldn't stop thinking that all these tests were not for me alone. Max was testing himself too. He was letting me get closer each time. It was as if behind the dark mask of the stranger was a heart as vulnerable as mine.

You complete me.

He had let it slip. What did he need with this elaborate show? And so I was introduced to his intimate habits, and sharing them brought us closer.

Mrs. Andrews showed me how to make the tea. I brought it to him and served him his cup, just as she told me he liked it. His special cup on the plain silver tray. It was domestic and simple yet perfect. I poured and prepared like a geisha might, waiting on her Shogun lord. *Service in the small things, Paula.* The little pleasures in life are divine.

The ritual of inspection: his hands on my body as he explored and caressed me, a possessive intimate touch. He inspected me for my physical health and my cleanliness and grooming. I was gone over by him minutely. He was complimentary and appreciative. He adjusted the line and hang of my clothes until I was perfect in form and symmetry. I was an object, yes, but I was *his* object, and I felt a pride in his undivided attention. He was spending precious time on me, making me a better girl.

Was that weird? Well, maybe! But what about the last few years when I was always taken for granted? When was the last time a man had given me the attention I had craved? I had never known the intensity of scrutiny to which Max had submitted me. A girl could do a whole lot worse than a lifetime of such ritual. I had felt as if I might burn up under the heat of his caresses.

Then he had gone for my ass.

It was vulgar and embarrassing. Intimate and hot. The contradictions of a taboo breached made me blush once more. Sure, I gave him muffled *no*'s, but my body wanted more. Did he know that? He wasn't listening. He took me once again.

I could have fought with him or objected more strongly, but I knew he was in control. Max didn't give me a choice, but I had wanted it anyway. *You decide when you come into my house*, he'd said. There would be no part of my body he did not know, that was what he told me. Then he touched me between the buttocks.

I had never had anal sex, and the stimulation back there was alien. I was curious, I admit; I read *Cosmo* and I'd seen a few pictures. Not always, but sometimes, I imagined a man there, bending me over and having me. I knew, of course, that my body was capable of doing such things without hurting. Yet I was unpracticed and unsure. The unknown always makes us apprehensive.

The sensation of his tongue and fingers there was entirely novel and not altogether unpleasant. It was different than being touched up front, not as sensitive but very sexual. The sin and dirtiness of the act made the experience breathy. To have my back place touched and stroked made me feel my shame all the more keenly. He would not let me hide. I could not even pretend it was not happening to me. Max spoke to me of his intent. He told me he was going to train me to take it, to later receive his cock in that tight back place that good girls shouldn't think of. He was going to mold me into his personal ass-whore to serve him with all of my body. The words themselves were as disgraceful as my pleasure at his intrusion. Where did that power and presence come from? His presumption that I would serve him. I was wet and weak at his words. He breached me with a finger tip and worked his knuckle in. I bore the plug he put in me and carried it all afternoon. The weight of it, and the sensation of being stretched, bound me to that man. What would Aunt Em say to that! Oh, what had I become?

The last of my humiliations was the ritual of The Binding. Where on earth did he get the ideas for all of those things he did to me? Were they in those dirty books in his library? All of these things he gave a name to. Recalling it, I lifted my shirt and looked at the flesh of my chest. I paid close attention to the area around my breasts for evidence of any marks that were left. There were none. They had faded. Just as Max – sir – had said they would. He knew what it would do to my body. He had roped me in a chest harness that encased my neck and breasts. It wasn't sore, but it was tight. It didn't stimulate directly, but it was sexy as all hell. Underneath my turtleneck he'd made me wear his creation. He had tied me up, the strands pressing my flesh, the hidden evidence that I was claimed. *Paula, girl, he roped you up like you do when you break a filly. And you wore it.*

He had kept my brassiere (that's one pair of panties and one bra – at this rate I'll soon have nothing left to slip on in the morning) and sent me home wearing the thing with instructions to keep it on. When I'd gone upstairs, I'd lifted my sweater and looked at what he had done: my naked breasts, nipples tight, framed in a rope cage. It would be nothing for him to tie my arms and pull on the harness to take me. It was his invisible hand that I felt on me as the rope pressed into my skin. I wore it all afternoon. I felt very close to him.

Slave.

Sex slave.

His finger inside my ass.

His rope around my breasts and neck. What was

I becoming?

God, I am wet. God, I'm so hot. I want to cram my fingers between my puss lips and finish what he's begun.

That day I had gone out; I had walked the streets and gone into the stores along with my Aunt Em. Everything looked normal, but I was a changed woman inside. I was a claimed woman. My desire was a groan between my legs, it ached for his rough cock. I wanted Max to push me down and take me more than anything.

I had unwound the rope before going to bed and run my fingers over the pattern it left on me. Max's touch on my skin. I had washed the steel bulb of the toy in my ass and hidden it all at the back of my closet. Was I meant to bring it back today? *What do I do with these things? Do I put them in that old shoebox along with my other life? Or do I start a new secret box for these treasures I have acquired?*

In my dreams last night, no one came to claim me. I knew the reason why. Last night I went to bed already claimed and I had given in. I curled up with my pillow between my arms and slept the deep sleep of the truly content.

CHAPTER 9
A CONVENIENT DISRUPTION

TEN TO ELEVEN.

What was I going to do?

There was a loud knock at the front door downstairs. Somebody was outside. I heard Aunt Em shuffle from the kitchen on her way to answer it. "I'm coming," she shouted after a second round of knocks. She answered the door; there was some discussion. I looked out of my window, but there wasn't a post van or a courier truck below.

"Someone here to see you, Paula. Are you coming down soon, girl?"

Someone here to see me? I checked the time. Stay or go? Max was expecting me. I put the rope and metal ass plug into a plastic bag and folded it into my purse. I would hand it to Maximilian and tell him I liked him, but that things were going too fast. I'd ask for my underwear back. A couple of dates and a couple more weeks; then perhaps I'd know what was happening. I just needed more time.

He was standing at the door.

"Sorry, Paula, there's been a leak. The plumbers are over there now. I know it's a bit of a disruption, but would you like to go out instead?"

Go out? I'd been planning to tell him it was on hold. That we should cool things for a while. That I'd had a swell time and he was attractive and wonderful, but it was moving way too fast. That I was a little worried – at myself, at what I'd become. That I wanted my pussy back if I'd given the impression it was okay for him to borrow it. No. That was not strictly true. But how could I tell him the truth? That I wanted him more than anyone I'd known, but I was afraid that I was falling too hard? That I needed to stop so I could regain my breath because I was scared of where this would go? Scared because it felt so good? Scared of how deeply I'd fallen for him? How could I have that conversation with him while Aunt Em was standing there listening? *Not in a million years, Paula girl!* I felt my ears starting to burn.

"Out? Sure. Why not?" I heard myself speak. I clutched my purse with its evidence.

"That's great." He touched my arm. "There's a couple of old bookstores behind the rail house road, down on Franklin Lane. There's a bakery in one. We can grab lunch while we're browsing."

"I like that shop, Paula dear, I go there myself with the Rotary. I always get the egg sandwich – they give you potato chips on the side." Aunt Em shooed me out and there wasn't room for refusing, and so it was that I found myself walking towards town with Max.

"It's a nice day. I fancy a stroll." He offered me his arm.

"What have you got Mrs. Andrews doing? Is she out with the bucket and mop?"

"She's very handy with a wrench, is Mrs. Andrews. You don't want to get on her bad side. Clonk you one she would, you know. She's keeping the plumbers in line."

I slipped my hand round his elbow and fell in at his side and we headed off together. He wore cuffed wool pants in a modish cut and Oxfords on his feet. He had a collared sports jacket of chocolate brown and, of course, an indomitable smile. Breaking up, I thought, could wait a day – for now I rather liked being out with my man.

There were no Max Broekners on the shelf of Second Life Books in Grand Falls.

"Where would they be hiding?"

"Usually in the Mystery section, but they sometimes hide them in Thrillers. I once came across one under New Age Philosophy, which tells you that not all book sellers read."

"They must be sold out." Between a Matt Minogue by John Brady and *Final Copy* by a guy named Brogan, the shelf was only conspicuous by a distinct lack of anything Broekner.

"Yes, I'm sure that's what it is. I suspect a bus load of Broekner fans showed up yesterday and scooped every last one. Happens a lot. What a shame." We both laughed at the idea of it. "And to think, I didn't bring a pen!"

"Well, why not? They could have, you know. Why not be famous that way?"

"A lesser mortal might blame the writing, but in my case it's entirely my agent."

"What?"

"He's awful. Truly. You'd hate him."

"Really? That can't be true, Max!"

"No. You're right. He's an angel. I don't know how he puts up with me. But I'm rubbish, I can't write at all, so what can the poor fellow do?"

"No, you're not!"

"I am. I'm terrible. And shameless! How would you know, anyway? You haven't even read one of mine. I tell you, Paula, I'm no good – first class no good for readers."

"You're just saying that." I squeezed his hand. "You're good enough for me, at any rate."

"A compliment? My, my. Are you trying to get on my good side? Well, keep it up because I think it's working." He kissed me. He tasted like capers and mayonnaise. "Perhaps I'm not entirely awful – there are a couple of characters I'm fond of. I do my best, it pays the bills, and it brings some people pleasure."

"Lots of people. And what's not to like about that?"

"My thoughts exactly, Paula. Come here, girl. And it is anything but boring."

"Perish boring."

"Life should never be dull."

"Do you ever write about other things? You know. Do your appetites find room on your pages?" I was close to him now. I slipped my hands inside his jacket and round behind his waist.

"Appetites? Why, Paula, whatever do you mean?" He raised a roguish eyebrow. "Do you think the readers want to hear how good egg sandwiches can be?" He pushed my hair back off my neck. My belly was pressed against his waist and I could feel him move a little. He backed me up against the bookshelves till my bottom was touching the books. He tilted his head, and his lips grazed my ear while he cradled my cheek with his left hand. "Or are you thinking of something else entirely? Something on a different menu?"

His lips caressed the side of my neck between my ear and my collar bone. He brushed my face with a stroke of his thumb while his right hand moved down lower. Down it moved, down the middle of my back till it took hold of my ass and squeezed it. He pulled me against him – I could feel him firm as he rubbed against my belly. I pushed my breasts against his chest while my hips moved to mount his thigh. I was out in my colourful Mary Janes, which gave me no heel for height. I went up on my toes as we writhed together, and then I rubbed my knee up his leg. I could feel his taut, heavy thigh muscles under the tailored cloth. My hand lingered. The strength of his frame against my body brought on a shiver of delight. The pressure of his leg against my untended puss was starting to get me off.

"Appetites, Paula." We were at the back of the store; there was no one nearby, and the place was nearly empty. The only other customer and the owner were both up front. He moved his hand up under my coat and gripped my breast and nipple.

"Take me," I whispered. I wanted him so. I had been aching for him since I woke.

"You want it, don't you?" It wasn't a tease. He was as aroused and hoarse as I was. "It's a need in you to be taken and held. You ache for the pleasure inside."

God, yes. I kissed him hard. I bit his lip and he reciprocated. He grabbed my wrist and pushed my arm wide, pinning it against the shelf. I jutted my hips out towards him and rubbed against him like a cat.

"You do. You want it. You need it. Don't you?" He looked down at my grinding crotch.

"Yes, sir." I heard my hushed voice tremble. It felt dirty to say it out loud. He let me go only to free his own hands with which he pulled at my blouse and undid me. He spilled my chest and exposed my breasts which he tumbled from my bra. He rubbed them and thumbed my nipples.

"Brazen whore," I heard him mumble before he grabbed my wrists again. He bowed his head to my bosom. I've always liked my breasts touched. He latched on a nipple and suckled me hard, biting and stretching.

I was lit up. It wasn't just his play with my breasts – his tugging, insatiable lips and his tongue generating currents of pleasure unbidden through to my womb – it wasn't just that, it was more. It was his taking of me, here in the store, and his restraining me by my wrists. He was having me and I could do nothing but love it; he was having me out in the open. I was helpless, pinned by his arms. He had forced me up against the bookcase and was undoing me out in public. Who might see? Who might come in? Who might hear a sound and investigate? There was a thrilling urgency to our possible discovery; I'd been uncovered and he was having his way. He held my wrists above my head and lifted the hem of my skirt. He unbuttoned himself.

"I'm going to take you here. I'm going to fuck you right here, right now, where anyone can find us." He kissed me forcefully and I took his tongue while he guided his stiffness to my panties. He held the thick knob of his ready erection as he fingered my elastic aside. I lifted a leg to aid his attentions. I wanted him in me ... and then he was.

It hurt a little. Just at first. He was dry to start, but my desire made him slick and soon he was inside me fully. His forehead and the top of his cock dragged blindingly across my clitoris. Poor little bud! Sensitive flower! He stepped on it like a brute. A brush of silk would have set me off, but his hammering made me feel faint.

He was taller than I was and though I stood on my tip toes, I was impaled and hung from his cock. I sat down on it like a balancing beam, with my legs draping down either side. He took my weight, his hand under my ass, and lifted me half from the floor. In and out, in and out, he drove me against the stacks. He liked to take it almost fully out, so I could feel my channel closing, and then when he had almost slipped from my folds, he would thrust back in without warning. Deep. Deep I felt him. He rutted me, pressing so hard that I had to part my thighs as he opened me. And I rode his girth as he withdrew again, my pearl tortured raw in ecstatic friction.

He fucked me, he did, my man Max; he fucked me just like that, standing up. My wrists were pinned by his hand above my hair and my chest exposed in front of him. He hefted my thigh and made me balance on one leg as he drove into me over again. He fished with his thumb and caught my hair, which he wound in and pulled till it hurt; he kept me pinned fast like that. There is something about being fucked with your hair being pulled that is shameful to admit you like.

He let my leg go; I found purchase on a shelf, one foot off the floor. He put his fingers around my throat.

"Kiss me, Paula," he whispered tightly, squeezing my neck gently. He was moving quicker, nearing his end, and my breath felt a little constricted. I couldn't move, so pressed was I by my man who was mounting me. I was pinned between the shelves behind and his chest in front, the feel of his hard heat inside me. He was gripping me tightly and urgently. And so it was, with our mouths vacuumed together, that I felt him release into me. He bucked and thrust and bucked again, and I felt the books move on the case behind me. His gush in my womb was the final straw and my own orgasm swept over me.

Like a boiling egg, trembling in the pan, the core of me started to rumble. It built and it built from behind my hood where my poor clitoris was touched and swollen. As one I felt it all connect – from his hand on my throat through to my centre, through my breasts and back up to my mouth. His leaden cock, soaking my channel, was spilling seed deep into my core. I pressed against his hold on me, but I could not free myself. It was everything I had always wanted – to be taken and to be held.

He was stronger than me. He wanted me. He had taken me and I was his. His warm semen ran down his erection and I could feel it start to trickle down my leg. He held me tightly as we both trembled together in the aftershock of our release. I felt his intrusion grow soft in me and I squeezed it to feel it still.

He withdrew.

I covered my chest, tucking my nipples and breasts back into my brassiere. It was only later that I noticed I'd misaligned the buttons on my blouse. I tried to arrange myself like a lady, covering up my cum-stained cunt. He had a handkerchief and wiped me clean; then went to attend to himself. I touched his wrists to stop him. I squatted down on my heels before him and I licked the residue from his penis. I pushed my tongue over his glans and through the gap at the top of his shaft. I lapped it up like a good kitten while his hand continued to stroke my hair.

I could feel my panties sticky. More of him came dripping out but got caught in the mesh of my lingerie. What a slut I was. I buttoned him back into his pants. The owner gave us a curious look as the bell rang on our way out the door. We were laughing like idiots and holding hands, acting like a pair of school kids. I let out a shriek when I caught sight of my hair in the reflection of the glass window.

THE NEXT DOOR DOWN, Better Books of Grand Falls, had two second-hand Max Broekners in stock. The lady who ran it wrapped them in paper and tied the bundle together with string. "I don't hold with all them plastic bags," she told us with conviction.

I held Max's hand and carried the parcel. I wanted to be holding a part of him.

CHAPTER 10
THE OTHER WOMAN

"CLOSE THE DOOR, PAULA."

I was in the room upstairs.

"Come stand near the end of the bed."

He was sitting on a plain wooden chair, black like his boots and his belt.

"Undress slowly. Everything off. Fold your clothes carefully and stack them neatly in one pile on the end of the bed."

It was two weeks after the bookshop. I always blushed when I found myself naked while he was fully clothed. I felt terribly exposed and kept my thighs pressed together while I crossed my arms over my chest. My skirt unzipped at the right hand waistband; my bra was the front-opening sort.

"Such modesty in a lady, Paula."

My panties were the last to go. They were French knickers, cut up to the hip, and black silk to match my new bra. I stood before him entirely stripped, waiting for what would now come. "Lie down over my lap." I might have mewed. I stood next to his legs and bent over his knees. I put a hand on the floor to keep steady.

He arranged me a little, pushing my hips a tad, till he had me just as he wanted. My bottom felt like a sailboat at sea, exposed with a storm on the horizon. My heart pounded. I squeezed my eyes shut.

Smack – smack – smack!

I parted my lips and gasped aloud as I writhed against his thigh. *Smack – smack – smack!* He wasn't letting up, and as I struggled he held me firmly down.

"Ohhhh!"

"What is it, Paula?" He touched my puss and rolled his fingertips over me in a circle.

"Oh sir!" With a pad of his finger either side of my clit, my juices started moving.

Smack – smack – smack! Again I was spanked; then his fingers once more in my puss. And so it went on for I don't know how long, but I know I cried before I came.

"MRS. ANDREWS?"

"Yes, dear?" She was holding the kitchen door open for me as I balanced the tea pot and tray.

"I was just wondering if everything got fixed – what with the sink being broken and all."

"Sink, dear?" She looked confused. "Whatever do you mean?"

"You know, the plumbers."

"Plumbers, dear?"

I almost spilled the tea when I laughed.

I WAS ON MY KNEES.

"Open."

I was upstairs in the room, on the carpet, while he sat on the edge of the bed. He unbuttoned his jeans and took out his cock and held it in front of my lips.

"Open your mouth and hold it. Slut."

I didn't need a second request.

We had been downstairs in his study when he'd called me over for my inspection. When he'd lifted my dress he found me in grey stockings with a lacy band at the top. I had been down in the town the day before and had picked a few pretty things. It seemed that Max approved. He had grabbed my wrist and dragged me upstairs and pushed me down on the floor. He was half firm before me and his cock was jumping as it did when he got excited.

"Oh, thank you, sir!" I kissed it. I closed my eyes and fished it into my mouth, feeling it warm and swollen against my tongue. It grew again and I pushed it into my palate as it reached to the back of my throat. I closed my cheeks about it snug and sucked back all of the air. With a tight bond of my vacuumed sealed lips, I licked him from helmet to balls.

"HI." I WAS AT THE OFFICE to which Max had given me the address. A well-dressed woman answered the door. I pegged her as forty, very assured and mannered; I figured her for one of the accountants.

"Legal counsel," she told me afterwards. She'd graduated summa cum laude.

"Oh, hi. Gosh. Is it that time already? I'm sorry, I'm running crazy. I got behind in my appointments this morning. Just give me a second, will you?"

I could hardly refuse. She collected a bag and coat from her manicured office and told reception to hold her calls.

"It's Paula, right? I'm really pleased to meet you." She had a genuine warmth and a smile. I couldn't help but take a liking to her even before she shook my hand. It was like old time friends catching up, which made our encounter all the stranger. She was the woman that I'd seen Max with the night he caught me peeking.

"Susan. Call me Sue. Everyone does. Come with me, let's both grab a coffee. I drink the fancy stuff." There was a faint touch of a soft accent in her speech, perhaps from somewhere down in the South.

It's funny when you meet someone you've been dreading for a while. It wasn't that I'd thought about her as competition, but I couldn't shake her from my impression of Max. He had either sensed this in me or had known intuitively that I harboured these questions about her. He had given me instructions to go and meet her; and like a good girl, I had obeyed. I didn't like it that I had to know, but I couldn't help myself.

"So what do you do, Paula?" Sue bought the cappuccinos and a couple of biscotti, which came on a china plate. We took them to a back table and sat down face to face.

"I'm sort of between jobs, I guess you might say. I was in marketing, but I was trying for nursing, and I think that's where I'm heading."

"Wow!" She was honest and enthusiastic, the sort who keeps cheering for a losing football team year after year after year. "How on earth do you marry those two? That would be the strangest degree I've heard of." She wasn't patronizing.

She was a good listener, and despite my anxiety and initial frosty thoughts, I found myself talking openly. She didn't judge, she was full of sound advice, and I could speak to her like a close girlfriend. It was better, even – I could let it out, and against my guard I liked her.

"So you have the biology credits from your freshman year? How many more are you missing?"

"I could finish it all in one year if I pushed it. I should have listened to my heart from the start."

"Someone talked you out of it?" And then we talked about boyfriends.

"I told all this to Max, and he listened like he does, and he's trying to convince me to do it. He says I should go back and work at something fulfilling and be the best person that I can."

"That's nice."

"You don't think he might be pushing me away?"

"Not at all, Paula, quite the opposite. Sounds like

he cares about you. The creeps of this world would want you to stay 'cause they'd feel threatened by you making good."

She was wearing a ring. I normally notice these things immediately, but I'd been caught up by her coat and her bag. Sue bought clothes from shops that wouldn't let me inside. Her heels would have cost a month of my old rent.

"You're married?" It just came out. I hadn't meant to embarrass her. Good thing, she wasn't at all.

"Of course, honey! Hasn't Max told you anything? No? Oh dear, then what must you think that I am?" She put her hands on mine, nails with a French polish, and gave a laugh that I found reassuring. "Paula, he told me that he's with you, and that you saw us – you know, doing it. Don't blush! So I guess you're wondering what was going on?"

I couldn't say a thing.

"You really are an innocent thing. Well, I'll see what I can do."

I was all ears. My biscotti hung inches from my mouth.

"I guess I've always known what kind of girl I am; perhaps you understand? What I mean is, I've known the sort of man that I like – the strong type with rough hands. Perhaps you like that too, Paula? I think likely so, otherwise you wouldn't be here listening today or hanging out with our author friend.

"You see, the thing, and you might have noticed it, that our needs – yours and mine – aren't really that rare. There are lots of women that go for a strong type of lover, a man that takes control and carries you away. Goodness, am I blushing or is it just hot in here? You don't have to say. It's me who's confessing, and you can judge if I'm right or wrong. What I mean is, there are lots of women that like the *idea* of it, but hardly any that get the loving they want.

"I don't mean I'm a doormat, Paula; in fact, I hate anything like that. I'm head of Legal and I got there by effort, by brains, and none of it by looks. I'm not saying a thing against equality of the sexes, but between the sheets I like a man to take control. I don't see that as wrong, and it's no one's business but ours, and I met the man of my dreams way back and he gives me the loving I crave.

"Don't look at me with those eyes, girl, I don't mean your Mr. Max. He's all right, but no, not for me. He's not the one I'm talking about. I met *my* man fifteen years ago and we've been happily married for twelve. I don't know if you understand or approve, but he's in charge of all things in the bedroom. Maybe you do understand? One of the things he likes me to do is go out with other men. I'm not complaining. I was told to talk to you and told to give it to you plain, so judge me as you see fit. I have all the power in my day-to-day, but come night time I like to be told. I like to be held and touched – treated like a lady and used like a dirty whore. What real woman doesn't? I don't know. Maybe I am a bad girl. I do confess that being spanked or tied up gets me more than a little excited."

After a sip of her frothy coffee she returned to her explanation. "Look at me! All self-conscious."

I couldn't say a thing.

"My husband's tastes – let's call them tastes – well, they're similar in some ways to Max's. Those two have known each other for quite a while and we've all got other friends. Well, sometimes I'm shared around."

I was squirming. The idea of being sent by your husband to other men made me slick with its shameful sin.

"It's not exactly a public thing, you don't bandy such things about, but I can truthfully say I feel as close to my husband as the day he gave me my collar."

"Collar?" A memory stirred at the word, something I'd seen in Max's study.

"Of course, sweetie. Oh, don't you know anything? It's the bond between a Dom and his submissive."

"What do you mean, a collar? Like for a dog?" I was interested, not critical.

"If you like. For some it is, for others it's sometimes less obvious."

"What's yours?" I was curious. Sue was indulgent and extended her leg and rolled her heel over to show me her ankle. I could make out the impression of a thin silver chain beneath her dark nylon hose.

"He owns me, my husband. I'm his. His slave, if

you like. He can do anything to me. Use me as he wants. I'm bound to him, I'm chained to him, and he takes me as he wants. God, I find that sexy."

I did too.

"You don't have to be married to wear a collar," she went on. "There are books that explain these things. Look it up on the net if you want, it's full of all sorts of perversions. The collar is sort of a game, but really it's not. It's the closest, most intimate thing ever. It means I'm his, and like I said, he does whatever he wants with me. He has me tied up and whipped by other men and fucked like you've never known." She gave me a flash of her bright white teeth. "Or maybe you do? Naughty Paula!"

I blushed.

"What I'm saying is, Max doesn't play around, but that doesn't mean he isn't amorous. Some of us – maybe you? – are more liberal-minded than others, and it can take you to fantastic places if you submit to your deepest desires. Oh, darling, you just wouldn't believe it! The things that I have done!"

"Are you happy?"

"I go to sleep with a smile every night."

BEFORE SHE LEFT, Sue picked up the notepad I had with me on the table.

"What's this, honey?"

"A shopping list. Max asked me to pick it up. He has something planned for the weekend."

"Really? Can I have a look?" She turned it over.

"That's all of it?"

"Yeah. Kind of weird."

"Ginger? That's all?"

"I think he's going to make me a Thai dinner or something of the sort. Or maybe he'll get Mrs. Andrews to do it for a special lunch."

"Honey, I don't think the cooking he has in mind has anything to do with Thailand."

"What do you mean?"

"Why don't I drop you at the store? I don't want to spoil your surprise. If you want, we girls can do a little shopping of our own and I can give you a couple of pointers."

I had come to her bitter with anxiety. When I left I had found a friend.

CHAPTER 11
THE SPICE OF LIFE

"YOU LOOK VERY PRETTY, PAULA."

"Thank you, sir. I try."

"Did you get everything I asked you for? Did you have any trouble?"

He walked around me as if circling prey, his eyes on me all the time. I found my new shoes a bit stiff – they'd take a little breaking in – but they were a perfect match for the skirt Sue had found. It was pleated but hung snug round my hips in a quality weave. Both were camel. I handed Max my paper bag, and he looked inside.

"Just as I asked." He withdrew the root of ginger. It was a large piece with many fingers, each twisted and bloated with juice. "Do you know what this is for, Paula?" He continued his parade around me. I noticed he stopped behind my back as if taking a look at my legs. Perhaps he'd been drawn to the black seam that ran up my flesh-coloured nylons? It had been Sue's suggestion – she was a bad influence –

to buy the garter belt and stockings. *They're perverts, the lot of them, God bless. A contrast seam up your hose and he'll dive into your petticoats*, she'd laughed. Max did not appear immune.

"You're cooking dinner?" I suggested.

"No, Paula."

"I'm cooking dinner?"

"Strike two. I'm going to trim it and peel it and bend you over, and I'm going to insert it into your ass."

I must have turned ten shades of red.

"I'm going to tie you up and make you take its heat, and I'm going to whip you while it's inside."

I think my legs shook. I could hear my heel tap like a telegram operator knocking out a message of distress.

"Don't worry, my dear." He stroked my face. "Don't worry about letting go. If I think you are likely to shout too much, I'll gag you before the end. And when I take the ginger out, it is only just the beginning, because today I'm not going to stop with that; today I will fuck you there." He put his hand on my clenched backside as if to reinforce his meaning.

Dear lord! I was to be sodomized! I was to be violated and disgraced with that hot root; my rectum intruded! I was to be shamed and buggered and whipped as well. Could he be serious? Could I turn and run in these high heels? And yet a warm tight knot in the bottom of my stomach told me that all would be well. I could see Sue's expressive eyes warm with mischief. The bad girl had known all along what Max had intended for me.

"Give me your hand, Paula."

I tried to remain calm.

"Fingers together. Turn your palm up."

He brought out a coil of climbers' rope, ruby red in colour.

"I'm going to lay the end of the rope half way up your forearm." He did so. "And then walk it towards your wrist."

I watched him as he counted it out.

"Like this. See? And when I get to the heel of your palm … "

He was fully clothed before me, and I somehow felt undressed.

"I'm going to start wrapping it around your arm."

Max rubbed his index finger over my palm before he started to coil the rope. Like a Gypsy palm reader, he traced the lines while looking into my eyes. He kept the loops tight against my wrist as he wove an elaborate bracelet. He wrapped the rope around and around me, encasing me like a snake. On the last turn, four inches up my arm, he doubled the rope back into a loop.

"Through the hole … " He spoke it like a remembered rhyme. It tightened up snugly when he pulled. "There. How does it feel? Secure?"

"Yes, sir." He tugged the rope and I felt its pull. I couldn't help feeling juicy.

"Do you think you can get away?"

"No, sir. I'm sure I can't." I didn't want to either.

He had taken to shaving me daily. He did it himself; I wasn't allowed. I had to hold my skirt or dress up for him while he lathered me with warm soap. If I was wearing pants he made me take them off, but had me keep my panties on. He'd pull them down around my knees and move them if they were in his way. He shook the razor in a bowl of hot water to clear it and keep it clean. He used a safety razor for most of me, but employed a straight one for parts hard to reach. I tell you this because being tied up made my puss run wet, and because it was smooth, like the rest of me, my juices trickled out.

"Try to get away."

"Sorry, sir?"

"Try to escape, Paula."

I pulled hard. His arm went with me, holding the rope, but the coils around my wrist held tightly.

"Do you see the end of the rope sticking out from the coils? The end that's nearest your elbow?"

"Yes, sir." It was obvious. The end of the rope stuck out from the loops that were coiled about my wrist.

"Pull on that with your other hand."

I did so and the whole apparatus slipped away. I was free. It was that easy.

"See? You can escape. If you can reach," he added.

He then undid his leather belt and slipped it from

its loops. I watched it slide with bated breath, anticipating its use. But Max, instead of hitting me, put it around my neck. The end went through the buckle, and he held it like a leash.

"Come with me, my pet." The leather constricted around my throat, and I was led upstairs to the room.

I was in the room where I had first seen him, all those weeks before. But now it was I who was bound with the rope and pushed down onto the bed. He flipped me over so I was face down and pinned me with his knees. My breasts were squashed underneath me and my head was turned to the side. I thought of his description of the ginger in my ass but couldn't quite believe it would happen. His belt was still around my neck but was no longer tight. He tied my right wrist to the bed frame so that my arm was fully extended – his strength was an unflinching thing. He tied my left wrist just as deftly and I soon found myself stretched both arms out, roped to the head of the bed frame.

"Pull on the ropes, my girl."

I pulled as hard as I could. The bed frame gave a gentle creak but showed no sign of weakness. The pressure on my wrists was spread through the coils and it was clear I was going nowhere. He reached under me and tore open my blouse and pulled my brassiere down. Acutely aware of the nakedness of my breasts, I felt my nipples become quite tender. I could feel his crotch and his thighs straddling me; he was only inches away from my ass.

"Pull on the end of the rope that will release you."

I couldn't reach it. I couldn't turn my fingers more than a couple of inches. I moved my head and tried to grab the end with my mouth, but I knew that it was hopeless. My arms were stretched long above my head and I couldn't reach further than my bicep. Max had tied me up and I wasn't getting away unless I could snap the rope.

"No luck?" Max got off me. I missed him already.

He sat on the edge of the bed and put pillows under my hips. He left my skirt covering my legs and took a hold of my ankle instead. He began to tie another rope. He fixed it to my ankle. Turned on from his confident touch and my enticing predicament, I began to grind my thighs together. In my heels and skirt I must have looked a sight with my ass propped up off the mattress.

What is it about being disarmed, being rendered helpless, that makes me want it so badly? It didn't help that I was writhing while Max was dressed and in control. He was staring at my body like a hungry man at the first course of a banquet. He fixed both my ankles with the ungiving rope, the other ends loose for the moment. I spread my knees to show him what I wanted. I was wanton with desire. I was giving him an eyeful if he wanted to look. I wanted him to raise my skirt.

Max reached up my leg and grasped my pussy in

his firm hand.

"Oh!" I moaned, and arched my back with desire, feeling his grip upon me.

I found my pleasure more difficult to come by when he tightened my right leg to the post. He let my puss go as I was stretched spread-eagled. He did the same thing to my other ankle.

"Much better," he commented. I needed him. I wanted it. I was tied to the bed like a prisoner.

It is a fascinating predicament to find oneself in, bound and at the will of another. The shutters were turned so we could get some light, but no-one could look in on us. I could feel the mattress beneath my elbows. I noticed Max had lifted something; like a stick of some sort.

Smack!

I screamed. The shock had taken me by surprise, and the pain was dreadful across my backside. Though I turned and squirmed and pulled as hard as I could, I could make no progress against my containment.

Max held the black leather riding crop balanced in his hand.

"Oh, sir!" I pleaded. He bent down to my ass and kissed my skirt where he had struck my haunches, then he raised my pleats like an opening curtain and threw them over my back. His tongue dragged along the rising red stripe that marked me where his switch had fallen. My new lingerie was stretched tight across my blushing behind. Sue's words floated back across my mind: *He'll like the garter belt — he's old fashioned that way. Just make sure you get a real one. Solid metal clips and wide garter straps and fully fashioned stockings.* Was this the attention she had imagined when she'd given me her advice? He kissed my ass. It was relief of a sort — his mouth on me — and yet a torment also.

It was no better to see the next strike coming. I tensed and tried to turn from the blow.

Smack!

He hit my other cheek, and I sobbed till he held me and sucked it, holding my ass in his hands. The sting of the whip, from its flared tip, had caught me flat on my rump. Sore. Sore! The sharp shock flattened out and left me with a dull hum. My nipples had stiffened, giving me away, if Max had cared to look. The shock and the pain mingled with a heat and the grinding discomfort of the mattress beneath me. I writhed against my bonds, twisting my legs, turning my elbows back and forth. I lifted my head and looked over my shoulder to catch a glimpse of the damage. Max licked his fingers and ran them over my mouth. He reached under and seized my nipples, holding them tightly.

"Oh! Oh, sir!"

He pulled them hard. My breasts contorted, tugged and pulled long by his hands. He let them go and they flattened again. He held my jaw and kissed me. He reached under again and kneaded my breasts and pulled my nipples and pinched them between his fingers. I tried to rise and when I did he put a finger inside my vagina.

"You're my girl now, aren't you, Paula? It was meant to be this way."

"Oh, sir." I wanted it. I didn't know what to say. He was teasing me to distraction. He held his finger inside my puss as he ran his riding crop over my skin. It was a gentle caress with the leather tip across the side of my face. Down my neck it went, on the outside of my breasts and across my flushed raised ass. He trailed the flared leather end between my legs and over my panty-pressed vulva.

"Oh sir!" I trembled – I could say nothing else – as he rubbed the end of it against my flower. Poor clit! So sensitive to this attention. I couldn't form the words for a conversation.

He smacked it.

"Uggggh!" I jumped. My body bucked with the pain and the torment. He'd whipped my pussy, landing his blow flat across my charms. I writhed as he returned his finger fully back inside me. He went down on me and licked it better, and I prayed he wouldn't stop.

"Keep it up. Lift your ass up. Stick your pussy out." I did so. "You'll take it, you slut. By the time I'm finished, you'll grow wet just at the sight of the thing. Kiss the end of it – go on, that's right, just as it gives you kisses in return."

He held the riding crop up to my mouth and I could do nothing but obey him. I kissed it, the fluttering leather wedge, as if it were my lover. He pushed the flared tip into my mouth and I held it between my teeth. The stiff leather was bitter against my tongue and the smell had a hint of me.

"Get it wet."

I licked it, obeying. He pulled it out my mouth.

Smack!

Once again on my bottom.

"Oh, sir!" And again on the other cheek, and he suckled me hard while he rubbed my puss with the riding crop again.

Oh, the twisted delight of the leather-wrapped crop playing across my folds! He ran it through me like a violin bow, back and forth between my contours. My juices gradually turned the shaft slick and made the black whip glisten. He followed my movements with the touch of his crop that he was using to masturbate me.

I pulled on my legs to escape the torment but was unable to move for the scarlet ropes. I could only twist my knees back and forth and arch my hips in my sweet anguish.

"Kiss it, Paula," he ordered me again and I could taste my own musk on the leather. I put my lips to the proffered whip and kissed it like a lover.

Smack!

I lifted off the mattress but came down quickly enough. My poor puss had taken a red sore swat and I felt my eyes go moist. I may have cried at this point, my tears obscured by my lifted skirt that Max had thrown over my shoulders. Two fingers he put into me now and with his thumb he massaged my clitoris. I was bound and exposed and under his hand and helpless to do anything but plead.

"That's it. Good girl. You're learning to take it now." He pressed the tip of the crop under my nipples as he continued to work on my cunt. Oh, Max! I was nearly there, did you know? I couldn't do anything but moan and sob.

He drew the crop across the top of my puss and down the inside of my thighs. He traced my garters and the top of my stocking and then followed the seam down my legs. He went from my knee along the line of my calf and then across the sole of my foot. He removed my high heels one at a time and stood them carefully by the bed. My toes were painted a dark cherry red; you could see them through the nude stockings. Max liked my feet looking pretty and I had wanted to please my man.

Smack!

"Ahhhh!" I shrieked; this one hurt most of all. He had struck the flat of my foot – whoever thought something could hurt like that? It was a new experience for me. He kissed it, soothing it, putting his lips to the black contrast seam which widened on the sole of my nylons. He sucked each of my toes in turn. Why was that so good? The sensation of his tongue trying to pry between my digits mingled with the lingering pain. My poor clitoris ached to be touched and welcomed shamelessly the return of the crop. Once again it was pressed flat to my flower and

I was able to grind on it hard.

Have you ever been undone? Have you ever given yourself over to a man to whom you are entirely helpless? Bound in rope and spread open? Made available to his desires? He can have all of you then, there is no stopping him, and that is what drove my dark lust. To be used. To be subjected to the discipline of his whip and the caress of his rough hand. To have my breasts and ass and puss marked by his crop and my nipples pulled hard and suckled. To have my puss tormented by the very whip that set my body on fire. And all the while I could do nothing more than pull hard on my unshakable bonds. The red rope bright against the white sheets and my man working me with his plans. I was taken, smothered, powerless, and complete – complete most of all. A blanket descended over me then and I felt safe, though I could barely breathe.

I had fallen into a warm safe place, another dimension in the room. As if the bed had swallowed me up and rolled me in the duvet with him. I was cocooned. Then sensation dragged me back.

I thought I could endure no more and that I was ready to burst. Max with his mouth around my toes as he rubbed my puss with his crop. Oh god! Why was that so hot? I bucked like a mustang at a rodeo or a patient being given a shock. Those ropes were as strong as Max had promised; I felt them pull at my ankles and wrists.

Max stood up and unzipped himself. He took his

cock and his balls from his pants. He let them hang there outside his clothes so I could see them in front of my face. *Take me, sir. Take me.* My mind was melting away, but he wasn't ready yet. He knelt on the bed, straddling my back, and stroked himself with his hand.

"Whose pussy is this?" He reached between my legs and put his whip to my clitoris, nudging it with the firm leather end of the crop.

"Your pussy, sir," I volunteered. I ached to feel him inside.

"And whose beautiful body is this?" He rubbed himself against my back, wrapping his penis in my skirt. He continued to bring me off with his riding crop, but I couldn't reach my release. I could feel the heat from his erection as he pressed it near my neck. I leaned into the crop to take pleasure from it; I shamelessly wanted more.

"Your body, sir. It's your body for whatever you want it for. It was yours when I came into your home. I am your dirty girl."

I had learnt the mantra. I had chosen to visit his house. When I crossed the door I became his. A toy, an object – his girl. I was a fuck thing, a bitch, a princess whore, I was all these things and more. I was a mélange of contradictions within the whole and each a pleasure to behold. His beautiful Paula and his greedy cock slut, the girl he could not do without. His ardour for me was sincere and evident, and I loved that he lost control. He could take of me as he wished for I had accepted his invitation. I could do nothing about it now. I rubbed myself hard against his crop; my heat became my all.

Oh, I was close! My breathing had changed. I was gasping and pulling air quickly. I trembled and shook, my hips vibrating with tension, as I pressed into the whip on my pussy.

"Yes, you are mine." His mouth was close to my ear. He took the crop away.

I almost sobbed with frustration.

He moved down again and licked me out, a great lapping tongue through my labia. I lifted my hips to offer him more and he put his teeth around my folds. He pushed a tight tongue to my channel as he thumbed my swollen pearl.

I turned my face to my shoulder and sobbed – he was keeping me near the edge.

"Mine to do with whatever I want." His length of his cock twitched with approval.

Max now climbed behind me on the bed and smacked my poor puss with his penis. Again and again he beat me with it, a loud slap against my skin.

"Oh sir! Oh sir!" I grew a little frantic, needing to be fucked. His cock was so close to me, touching me, the very thing I desired most of all.

"This is what you want, isn't it? You filthy dirty whore."

"Sir!"

"You're a cock slut, Paula. Aren't you? You want it stuffed inside your cunny." He was rigid hard and coarse with me, which just made me want it more. "Cock slut," he taunted me in his gravel voice that spoke of his primal desire. "You want to feel my thickness, don't you? You want my cock rammed home."

"Sir!"

"You want to feel it scraping your womb and pumping inside you."

"Oh sir!"

"Say it, slut – that's what you are."

"I am!"

"What are you?"

"A slut! I'm a cock slut, sir, I am."

"What do you want most of all?"

"I want to be fucked by your big thick cock! I want to feel it inside my cunt!"

There is a therapy in such degradation, but it comes at a later time. It is when you are wrapped in bed beside your lover or you sit reading tucked under his arm. It comes when you look out of the window on a chilly, windy day. It comes upon you as a warming truth, a surprise from deep in memory. Those times are the best. When such admissions are truly special. When you recall with a smile the shared truths that will ever be bonds in your heart. He has pried your secret out of you and you wear his names with pride. Dirty names. Filthy names. Shameful to be spoken. I am his cock slut. I am his whore. I will know this all my life. It marks me more permanently than a tattoo, the knowledge that I am his.

"Sir?" I waited. "Sir?" I asked again. He pulled my panties aside.

The red jewel of my plug was visible to him now. He had made me wear it today, he had told me to, and Sue had reaffirmed the importance of obedience. *He's taking the time to show you attention – he's thinking about you through these things.* Max put his thumb and finger on either side of the toy and moved it back and forth. My ass muscle gave a purr at the attention.

"Are you growing used to your steely friend?"

I knew what he meant. Putting it in had flustered me for the first couple of days that I'd worn it, but now all it took was a dab of lube and then I squatted and slipped it in. I always knew when it was there. It could never be forgotten. I was always keenly aware of its weight that I carried inside my body. The solid steel warmed to me and I could feel it press inside my anus. I could feel it press through to my other side when I touched my puss or I was peeing.

When Max had first fucked me wearing it, I'd felt full, like I might burst. I hadn't, of course, and now I found it very satisfying – the complete sensation of 'filled.' More than that, it was an emblem of our sin: a totem of what I had become.

He turned it a little and gave it a pull that gave my ass ring a tug. The sensation of being vacated was a little alarming and brought the embarrassment of being on display. He got his face right down to it and watched as he drew it out. I had no secrets anymore; that is what I had become.

"Ooooh!" I let out a half stifled moan as I sometimes do when I'm opened by him in this way. An intrusion or a contraction there is often a breath-catching moment.

Max laid his crop aside. He wrapped one arm around my waist and licked a finger on his other hand. Around and around my tight back ring he touched and stroked. I let his trimmed fingernail in and he took me up to the knuckle. I was slightly ashamed at how easily I opened, but it gave my Max great pleasure.

"Very good, Paula. You're getting better all the time. Your training is going very well. And now I think you are ready."

He got off me and wiped his finger on a tissue. He went over to a small table and brought the whole thing closer to the bed. It was too short to be much use for anything – Alice might have brought it back from Wonderland.

It had a drawer.

Max opened it up.

There was a short chopping board inside it. And a paring knife.

"Oh, sir!"

And my lacy panties.

He gagged me. I recognized them – they were definitely my panties – the pair he'd taken from me the first day I'd gone over. They smelled clean and fresh, certainly laundered – had Mrs. Andrews done this for Max? He pushed them into my mouth. I almost choked, but he forced my jaw open till I took them. Luckily I could breath fine through my nose, but the sensation was quite disarming. I would have spat them out but Max was prepared for that. In the tiny drawer of the table was my brassiere. Like my panties it was clean and fresh, which I could smell as he tied it round my mouth.

I was gagged with my own panties, held in place by my bra round my head. I could only make moaning, throaty sounds that were muffled and indistinct. My eyes must have conveyed my alarm.

"I don't need to hear your shouting. You may be tempted to ask for release, but you aren't going to get it." He held up the fingered root of ginger I had brought for him in the bag. "A harmless root, a rhizome of ginger, with the ability to convey great sensation."

He was going to put it into my ass! He hadn't been kidding after all! I squirmed and I shook and shouted out. *Oh please God, don't let it be so!* But he was deaf to my protestation. I was trussed and bound by my arms and legs with my ass on display to all.

Yet I had only Max. He was the one I wanted. He was engaged in cutting and shaping the ginger and had left me to squirm with my private thoughts. I had never had anything in my backside before except for the toys and fingers of Max. I liked spiced, flavoured food, and in the city I'd gone for sushi. I knew the tang that ginger had; what could it do down there? I twisted and groaned in panic.

Something of the shape of the stainless steel ass-plug gradually emerged. It was the size of an egg, as Max carved it out, with a prominent tapered neck. The sculpture had an end to it like a large button off a coat.

"That's to stop it from all going all the way in." Max had caught my eye. He drew the knife over the coarse fibred flesh and I could see the juice leak from the bulb. How hot were those flavours that Max was promising to put inside my back passage?

"Are you ready, my dear?"

I wasn't going anywhere. I think I started to cry. Max bent down and put his tongue to my anus and licked it around and around. Oh, that was fine!

"Not too wet. Enough that it goes in easily. Then its own juices will give you a burn. Are you ready, my beautiful girl? I'm going to put it in." He was enjoying this! His cock was hard enough.

I didn't feel it at first. The fire. I felt the nudge of the ginger root just as I would the ass plug, and I responded just the same. I felt my rear door pucker and tighten, and then give in to his persistent attention. My sphincter widened and slipped snugly over the root, which felt cool after Max's warm tongue. I widened and stretched with each persistent nudge that was unbearable till he withdrew it, and then finally with a playful tap he slipped it passed the equator. The bulb's girth was more in than out, and then my ass muscle tightened and pulled the ginger completely into me.

It was slightly warm. An irritation. A warm breeze from somewhere inside me. Then it got stronger. And it didn't stop.

"Urgggh! Urgh!" I was reduced to grunts. I rocked back and forth and tried to push the thing from my anus. The heat was such I thought I was seared, and I feared it had done me damage. I heard my sobs, my broken wails, my failed and futile protest. Max was heedless – he took up his belt and drew my leather leash tight round my neck.

It was an eternity, yet ten minutes at most, as he rode me like a sled dog. He kept his belt leash tight so that it pulled on my throat while he whipped my ass red with his riding crop. Oh the burning heat of his stinging switch and the root that inflamed me from within! I'd have shrieked the house down if I wasn't gagged, and I only wanted it expelled.

He licked my ass, he kissed my ring, he got ginger on his lips. He roughly finger-fucked my desperate puss as he spanked me from behind.

And then it was over. It had been impossible to come. The distraction of the hot coal in my anus had deprived me of my pleasure. Max oiled himself up and set his cock to my back door and I was too weak to protest at his intrusion.

I was so relieved to have it out, that torment of vegetable heat, that I took his girth and length without protest. But his physical fulfillment inside my rear passage warmed me in another way. I became aware and then gasped for air. *He. Was. Fucking. Me.*

In. The. Ass. Oh, sir! He wrapped his hands around my garter straps and pulled on my stockings for everage. He drove me like a beast while his hand reached around and I felt the pleasure of his fingers in my flower. So worn was I by his earlier assault that this attention felt like delicate love-making. And I was full. Full like I'd never been. The pressure I felt from his subterranean intrusion was filling me in different ways. Out he almost came and then ran full into me again. I was his tied-up slut with my ass in the air and my skirt thrown over my head. He buggered me, his willing sodomite, taking his cock where no good girl would ever admit it. Yet I knew that this intimacy was only one more step in what I had wanted all of my life.

I came before him, tears in my eyes, relief that I'd been allowed my salvation. My thighs and arms trembled and gave out, and I lay still with the weight of him on me. He was locked in me, my ass grabbing him tight. I wouldn't have had it any other way. I would have kept him locked in me forever. He had come; I had heard his cries. And then he held me quietly. He kissed my shoulder. He called me his beautiful girl. His arms and legs entwined about me and he promised to never let go.

CHAPTER 12
A CIRCLE HAS NO END

"WHAT TIME IS YOUR TRAIN, PAULA?"

"Four thirty."

"You have your ticket?"

"Safe in my bag. I've only checked three times."

"Is that your aunt coming now?"

"You had best take your lovely hand off of my ass, then, and give me a kiss in a hurry."

I hugged Aunt Emily as she ran up to me, just as we'd done that first day.

"Oh, Paula, dear, my special girl! I can't really believe that you're going."

"Oh, Em, I'll miss you! Don't cry."

"How are you doing, Emily?"

"Just fine, Max. I didn't really think she'd go through with it. I thought you could convince her to stay."

"It's not so far, Em." I offered consoling words, but I was choking up already. "Max said he's coming to visit me, and I can get back for the occasional weekend."

"She's only got a year in the city till she's finished with those courses. Your beautiful niece will be back before you know it, and she's doing what's best for herself."

"I just don't think it's right, I don't care what you say. Girl split up from her man like that and leaving her family behind."

"Only for a little while," I reassured her, "and we're not really apart."

"What's that you're wearing now?" Em saw what I had on.

"You like it?"

"Kind of pretty. But isn't it a bit old-fashioned, or is that the new look now?"

"It's a choker and a cameo. Max bought it for my … as a present." I thought back to the previous night when he had opened the box and shown me, and how I had cried, overwhelmed with my feelings, as he'd fastened it around my throat. *Now you wear my collar, Paula.* I had slept with it on, nestled in his arms.

"I know what it is, girl, a band round your neck, I'm just saying it's a bit old style.

"I think it's perfect," Max squeezed my hand.

"So do I, my darling." I reached up and stroked the smooth dark velvet and knew I belonged to him.

"Well, whatever pleases you. But I still think this whole thing is mad. In my day you just went off and got married, and that was the end of that."

"I'll be back, Em, don't worry. And I'll write."

"See that you do, Paula dearest." Max kissed me as my train drew in.

I WROTE THIS AS A TESTAMENT to a time I will never forget. Little did I think, when I returned to Grand Falls, that my life would utterly change. Where once I was hollow, now I am full. Where I doubted of the existence of love, now it holds me tight in its grip. I am no longer the innocent girl; I am blissful, complete, and knowing. He has opened my eyes to the world.

I am his and I have flowered.